"Tandy, there are **Click took a shaky breath.**

"No." Her voice razor sharp, she threw up a hand.

"Tandy—"

"We're not talking about the past." The words were harsh.

He gritted his teeth. "Let me apologize."

She shook her head, her eyes narrowing. "It doesn't matter."

"It does, dammit," he argued.

"You need to apologize so I need to listen?" She shook her head. "So *you* can feel better? Be able to let go and move on?"

He tore his gaze from hers, staring at the floor. If he thought she was happy, that she'd moved on, he'd let it go. But she hadn't. And neither had he. Maybe together they could find a way back to living without bearing so much pain.

He sucked in another deep breath and stared at her.

"Have you?" He crossed the room, needing to be close to her. Yearning for her touch. "Because I can't...and I don't want to."

Dear Reader,

I'm so excited to share Click and Tandy's story with you. As a hopeless romantic, I like to believe that true love really does conquer all. Sometimes the obstacles are small. For Click and Tandy, that's not the case.

With most of Tandy's relatives falling in love and starting families, she's reminded of everything she had—and lost. Instead of getting bogged down in grief, she jumps on a too-good-to-pass-up job offer and the change of scenery it brings. But her past followed her to the West Texas town—and so does the heartache.

Click Hale hadn't planned on being a single father. But his daughter is all he has in the world, and he's determined to do the best he can. If he can win back Tandy's love, he'll give his daughter the family he never had and make his dreams come true.

I hope you enjoy our first visit to Fort Kyle and the rugged beauty of West Texas. Be on the lookout for the next Boone book, and happy reading!

All the best,

Sasha Summers

COWBOY LULLABY

SASHA SUMMERS

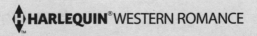

HARLEQUIN® WESTERN ROMANCE

ISBN-13: 978-1-335-69951-0

Cowboy Lullaby

Copyright © 2018 by Sasha Best

Printed in U.S.A.

Sasha Summers grew up surrounded by books. Her passions have always been storytelling, romance and travel. Whether it's an easy-on-the-eyes cowboy or a hero of truly mythic proportions, Sasha falls a little in love with each and every one of her heroes. She frequently gets lost with her characters in the worlds she creates, forgetting those everyday tasks like laundry and dishes. Luckily, her four brilliant children and hero-inspiring hubby are super understanding and helpful.

Books by Sasha Summers

Harlequin Western Romance

The Boones of Texas

A Cowboy's Christmas Reunion
Twins for the Rebel Cowboy
Courted by the Cowboy
A Cowboy to Call Daddy
A Son for the Cowboy

Harlequin Blaze

Seducing the Best Man
Christmas in His Bed

Visit the Author Profile page
at Harlequin.com for more titles.

For Jolene Navarro

Thank you for your time, your mad plotting skills
and your constant support.

Chapter One

"Lynnie would be spitting nails if she knew everyone in town had been here with the house looking this way." Tandy stood in the front parlor, surveying the room. Her massive dog, Banshee, sat at her side.

Most of the residents of Fort Kyle had already left, leaving casseroles, desserts and treats to cover Lynnie's kitchen counters and tables. Not that there was anyone left to eat them. Still, it's what folks did—bring food, visit, share memories that honored the recently deceased.

Tandy swallowed hard. It was difficult to accept Lynnie was gone. She'd been such a strong spirit, and Tandy couldn't imagine life without her.

Walking into Lynnie Hale's house was like stepping back in time. Any second now, she expected Lynnie to walk around the corner—wearing her favorite apron, with a welcoming smile on her face and stories to tell.

A wave of nostalgia rolled over Tandy. This had been the place she'd been happiest. Seeing it empty and quiet was plain wrong. She ran her fingers along the fine layer of dust on Lynnie's upright piano, a sure sign the older woman hadn't been home in some time. If she had, her piano would have stayed clean and neat. Lynnie Hale was—had been—fiercely and unapologetically house proud. To have the people of Fort Kyle here seeing her home and treasures in anything less than perfect condition would make Lynnie ashamed.

She hurried into the kitchen to find her cousins, Scarlett and Renata, covering food and storing it in the refrigerator.

"Anyone left?" Renata asked her.

"A few of her friends are still chatting in the living room. I think everyone else has cleared out," she answered, offering them both a smile.

"Can we clean now?" Scarlett asked.

"Bothering you, too?" Tandy asked. "I kept imagining her, how mad she'd be."

Renata nodded. "I only wish we could have set the place to rights *before* all of Fort Kyle came by."

Tandy nodded. No point wishing what could have been. "We can fix it now," she said, collecting a trash bag.

They cleared away the used dishes, stopping to chat with Lynnie's closest friends now and then. When the dishes were gone, Tandy pulled out a duster, wood polish and an old rag and got to work. Banshee trailed after her, her constant shadow. Renata was sweeping, and Scarlett took the trash out.

Grief sat heavy on her chest, but Tandy fought it. Lynnie wouldn't want tears or despair, she'd want laughter. Better to think about the dozens of homemade cookies, muffins, pies and breads they'd made in Lynnie's kitchen, the sticky-sweet jams or veggies they'd canned, or the hours upon hours Tandy and her cousins had spent playing the piano and singing at the top of their lungs. Lynnie wasn't kin, but she'd welcomed Tandy and her cousins into her home as if they were. Whenever they wandered onto her property—which was often—she'd gone out of her way to carve out time for them. So much love. And laughter. And music. Always music.

Lynnie's place was comfort and love, laughter and songs, and family.

Tandy surveyed her work, satisfied.

She turned her attention to the framed photos decorating the wall behind the piano. She ran the feather duster around each frame, each image a familiar glimpse at the woman they'd lost. Lynnie, tall and thin, in a handful of committees and board photos. Lynnie with her prized preserves, judging livestock shows and riding drag rider at the rear of a cattle drive. There were pictures of those Lynnie loved there, too. Tandy's picture was there, young and smiling, with Scarlett and Renata.

And Click. She studied his smile. Those blue-green eyes had made the world a better place. But that had been a long time ago.

Aaron "Click" Hale was part of her past. That's where he needed to stay. Her cheeks grew hot, her chest heavy. He'd turn up soon. Of course he would. For Lynnie. They were kin, through thick and thin.

I can do this.

Tandy headed back into the kitchen to stow her cleaning supplies. Inside her well-organized pantry hung Lynnie's collection of aprons. Some she'd made, some she'd bought and some were gifts. A rainbow of colors and shapes. Some were practical, the ones Lynnie wore daily. Others were pure silliness—with ruffles and sparkles and silly sayings. Still, Lynnie had held on to them.

Lynnie's favorite, blue calico and patched so many times the original fabric was suspect, hung aside. Tandy stroked the soft fabric, drawing in an unsteady breath. *I will miss you so, Lynnie.*

"Tandy?" Scarlett called out. "I'm putting on a pot of coffee for Widow Riley. Want some?"

Tandy closed the pantry, shutting away the memories and sadness that followed. "Sure."

"Think she'd be satisfied?" Renata asked, hanging the broom on its hook by the back door. Her blue eyes scrutinized their hurried cleaning efforts.

Tandy giggled. "I can hear her now. 'Dust is just a country accent.' Wasn't that it?"

Scarlett and Renata laughed. It was true. In West Texas, dust was part of the decorating. Best you could do was keep it to a minimum. They'd done that.

"Banshee," she said to the Anatolian shepherd. "Go outside for now." She rubbed him behind the ear as he passed, looking insulted by his banishment. "It won't take long," she promised.

Scarlett carried a tray with coffee into the dining room. Renata followed with a plate of cookies. If Lynnie's friends needed to stay a bit longer, they'd do what they could to be hospitable. It's what Lynnie would have wanted. They served coffee, cleared more plates and moved into the parlor.

"You should play something." Scarlett nodded at the now dust-free instrument.

She stared at the piano. "I can't," she confessed. "I don't want to embarrass her, crying on her keyboard."

Scarlett draped an arm around her shoulders. "I'm sorry this happened now. Not saying there's a better time for…" She broke off and shook her head. "You just moved here, is all I mean. To lose Lynnie now, when you're back, it's not fair."

Tandy nodded. Lynnie had played a huge part in her decision to move to Fort Kyle. She swallowed.

"Lynnie would be glad you were back, Tandy," Renata said. "And glad we set the place to rights."

Tandy nodded, her gaze sweeping the parlor and the

small group of white-haired ladies chatting away. Lynnie didn't have family to come and tidy up her place. Other than some second cousin in the city—which city had never been specified—Lynnie didn't have much.

Except for Click.

Tandy swallowed the razor-sharp lump in her throat, painful all the way down. Her attention wandered, but there was still no sign of Lynnie's great-nephew. He'd be hurting, too. Lynnie was his rock, the only family that treated him like he was more than a nuisance and mistake.

"How old were we?" Renata asked, studying the wall of pictures she'd dusted earlier.

She glanced at the photo of them. "Young." That girl hadn't imagined her future like this. That girl had believed in the promise of a future full of everything she'd never had.

"You okay?" Renata asked, nudging her.

"We don't have to be here." Scarlett took her hand.

"Of course we do," Tandy argued. "We all loved Lynnie. He might not even be here—"

"He's not," Scarlett said. "Not yet. Dad's been on the lookout for him."

Tandy looked at her. "Why? If I remember correctly, Uncle Woodrow was never very fond of Click."

Renata snorted. "Understatement of the year."

"But, now that Lynnie's gone, what will happen to her property?" Scarlett asked.

Tandy frowned. "The land?" She sighed. "Lynnie's been gone, what, three days? Uncle Woodrow's already worrying over her land?" Of course he was. That was the way he worked.

Scarlett wrinkled her nose. "*If* Mr. Wallace bought this place, Dad would have a heart attack."

Knowing her uncle Woodrow, that was probably true. Woodrow Boone, Scarlett's father, was...prickly. He excelled at voicing his opinion loudly and being contrary. Still, Tandy respected her uncle. What he lacked in charm he made up for with determination. If he was determined to keep Lynnie's place from falling into Vic Wallace's possession, nothing would get in his way.

Apparently, that was something that hadn't changed in Fort Kyle: Woodrow Boone v. Vic Wallace feud. The patriarchs of the two largest West Texas ranching families kept things civil in public—barely. The two men disagreed on everything. From cattle—Wallace's Angus versus Uncle Woodrow's Hereford—to fences—Wallace's stone versus Boone's traditional wood and wire—if they could find a way to disagree, they did.

Tandy had always thought Lynnie's place the prettiest in the region. The natural spring that bubbled up cold and clean was a huge bonus in the dry, arid landscape. But there was more to it than access to water. Lynnie's property was wedged between the Boones' and Wallaces'— a hot and arid Texas Switzerland between two warring families. And since Lynnie had outlived three husbands with no children to pass the land on to—

"Click will inherit," Tandy whispered, that realization making the tight grip on her control slip.

"Poor Click," Renata whispered.

"That's what Dad's waiting on." Scarlett shrugged.

Tandy leaned against the piano. Would he sell or stay? This place had been special to them all once, but now...

Renata glanced at Tandy with unfiltered sympathy. "I guess Click selling is what we want? I'd think having him around would be challenging."

Renata's words cut her deep. "I want him to be happy." That hadn't changed. But, yes, having him around would be *challenging.* Especially since she'd planned on making Fort Kyle home for a while.

"Are you sure you're going to be okay?" Scarlett asked. "If he shows up, I mean?"

Tandy forced a smile. "I'm fine. Completely and totally." Which was a complete and total lie. Neither of them knew the extent of the damage between her and Click, and she intended to keep it that way. No point dragging that nightmare out into the open for everyone to suffer through.

"As long as you're sure." But Scarlett didn't look convinced.

"We're here for Lynnie." Tandy looked at them both, hoping her voice didn't give away just how hard it was to say his name. "Click is your friend. I don't want that to change because of me. He'll need friends right now, so you should be there for him." She meant it.

She saw the doubtful look Scarlett and Renata exchanged.

"Tandy, Lynnie loved my pineapple upside-down cake," Miss Francis, Lynnie's dearest friend, said. "Had to bring some. You mind cutting some old ladies a piece?"

Tandy smiled, leading Miss Francis into the kitchen. "Not at all. Not that I see any old ladies around."

"Don't know what we'll do without her. She knew how to keep things organized—and the menfolk in line." The woman sniffed, pressing a hankie to her nose.

"She had plenty of practice with that," a deep voice said from the doorway. "Keeping the menfolk in line."

Tandy didn't have to look to know who was talking. She knew. Her reaction to him was the same. Her heart kicked into overdrive, and every inch of her seemed to tighten. Until the cold set in, soaking up everything until she was numb. It was easier that way.

"As I live and breathe, Click, look at you," the woman gushed. "Does an old heart like mine good to see you here today."

"Good to see you, too, Miss Francis."

Tandy sliced into the pineapple upside-down cake, putting pieces on the flowered dessert plates she'd pulled from Lynnie's china cabinet. Her hands were shaking, but there was nothing she could do about it. If she looked at him, it would be worse. So much worse. She wiped her palms on a kitchen towel and put the plates on a serving tray.

Any minute now he'd say something to her and she'd have to acknowledge him. She'd have to look at him, smile and act like seeing him didn't drag her straight back into the hell she'd been living in for the last two years. The hell she'd only just managed to bottle up and bury deep inside.

The silence in the kitchen grew thick and heavy, pressing in until she almost bolted from the kitchen. No more running. She swallowed, picked up the tray of cake slices and headed for the door.

"Click," she said, as close as she could come to a greeting. She slipped through the kitchen door, holding her breath when she brushed past him. Her lungs were aching by the time she reached the parlor and Lynnie's waiting guests. Even as she said his name, she couldn't bring herself to look at him. She was stronger now, but not that strong.

CLICK WANTED TO punch something. Over and over. Until the pain in his hand overshadowed the pain in his chest. Which would never happen. He wasn't sure he could do this. Hell, he'd arrived here feeling that way, barely treading water. That was *before* he'd known Tandy was here.

Now…the odds were stacked against him.

Her scent hung in the kitchen, the ripple of her skirt against his jeans waking his senses up. Every instinct told him to go after her. He wouldn't. He'd no right. He couldn't hurt her, hurt them, not again. He wouldn't survive it this time.

Her hazel-green eyes never looked at him. He should be relieved. Instead, the hole in his chest ached. He blew out a deep, slow breath.

"Looks like you never outgrow some hurts," Miss Francis said.

Click looked at the older woman, comforted by the presence of Lynnie's favorite cohort. "Ma'am?"

"Click Hale, don't you pretend you don't remember. Lynnie was plum tore up over what happened between you two. I know you were young'uns, but that doesn't mean you didn't love each other." Miss Francis shook her head. "Doesn't look like Tandy's forgotten either."

No, he hadn't forgotten their summer together. Those were cherished memories, long before the heartache of two years ago. He treasured each remembered smile, kiss and sigh. His heart had been whole and fearless, full of purpose and hope. He'd grown up since then.

Miss Francis patted his hand on her way from the kitchen. "Glad you're home, son."

He nodded, hooked his thumbs in his belt loops as Renata joined him in the kitchen. He looked at her, waiting.

She held her hands up. "Tandy told us to be nice to you. So I will. For now." She crossed the room, her hands rubbing his arms. "But don't think I don't have questions. Lots of questions."

He nodded, not in the least surprised by Renata's words. Of course Tandy would have told them to be nice to him—that was her way. She put others first, always. He cleared his throat.

"I'm so sorry about Lynnie," Renata whispered.

"Me, too." Lynnie had been too bighearted and too important to die. How could she leave him, now, when he needed her more than he'd ever needed anyone in his life? What was he supposed to do without her straightforward advice and guidance?

"How's life been treating you, Renata?" he asked, trying to get out of his head and away from his troubles—for a few minutes.

"Life's good, Click." She smiled.

"I'm glad." He grinned. He wanted only good things for her. He could count the positive forces in his life on one hand. Renata Boone was one of them. "Stonewall Crossing?"

"Growing." She shrugged, laughing. "Thanks to my brothers, all settled family men. Toben, too."

His brow shot up. Tandy's twin had been more inclined to take things one night at a time. "Toben? That's hard to believe."

She nodded. "I know. Boy, do I know. But it's true. And he's happy. What about you?"

Happiness had always been a foreign concept to Click. But he was trying. He had a very good reason to try. A reason he needed to collect from Widow Riley before all hell broke loose. "Good," he forced the word out.

Tandy.

Desperation gripped him. She didn't deserve to have this sprung on her—like it had been sprung on him.

"Better get out there," he said, catching Renata's confused look before he pushed through the kitchen door and down the hall.

He spied Widow Riley the same time Tandy did, and

froze. In the week since little Pearl's mother had placed her in his arms and left, since he'd learned he was a father, Click felt like he'd been driving ninety miles an hour down an endless pitch-black highway. Now Click realized that highway led him here, toward a horrible, inescapable collision. When Widow Riley had offered to rock Pearl while she slept, he didn't resist. Widow Riley had experience and confidence, two things he lacked when it came to babies. But seeing the old woman rock his baby girl, while Tandy approached—wearing her sweetest smile— had his stomach in knots.

"Who is this little doll?" Tandy asked.

Click braced for impact. He forced himself to move, to think, to remain calm. He'd loved Tandy since he was seven years old. It was one of the few constants in his life. That didn't mean she gave a damn about him. Still, his daughter's presence, her age, was bound to wound her deeply.

"This little angel is Pearl," Widow Riley said, still rocking. "Isn't she precious?"

Tandy placed her tray on the side table and crouched by the rocking chair. "She is that."

Click looked at his daughter. She was beautiful. She was also small, fragile and just as confused by his presence as he was by hers. The difference was, he was supposed to be responsible for Pearl.

"How old is she?" Tandy asked, her finger tracing one round cheek.

Widow Riley looked at him for the answer.

"Fourteen months." Click cleared his throat, his heart shuddering.

Tandy jumped up and knocked the tray, sending the remaining cake plates to the ground. He stooped to help her when Pearl started to wail. Pearl—his daughter and his obligation. He reached awkwardly for the baby girl, her slight weight in his arms still alien.

As far as babies went, she was pretty easy. She didn't cry often, and when she did, a few pats on the back seemed to calm her. A fact Click was thankful for. Chances were, he'd fought back more tears this week than Pearl had. He held her now, whispering to her softly, fully aware that all eyes were on him.

Again.

Seemed like his branch of the Hales couldn't turn up in Fort Kyle without causing an uproar. Not him so much, but his parents. This time, it was on him. Not that he gave a damn about what these people thought—not at the moment. The only person he owed any explanation to was on her knees, cleaning up cake and china from Lynnie's hardwood floors.

He'd imagined a dozen scenarios for their reunion. None of them included a funeral or a baby. Shame burned his face and neck. He couldn't bring himself to look at Tandy. He couldn't.

"She's yours?" Renata asked, kneeling to help Tandy.

He nodded, his throat too tight to speak.

The congratulations that followed were a surprise. For years, his presence had been greeted with judgment and gossip. He was no longer a child, but history had his defenses up. Lynnie had been his champion, shushing the whispers and gossip his sudden arrival on her doorstep was sure to kick up. What he wouldn't give to have her here now.

Never in his life had he felt so damn alone.

Pearl hiccuped, sniffed and burrowed against his shoulder. He held her, his hand spanning the width of her back as he cradled her close. "It's okay, Pearl," he whispered, patting her.

"She's beautiful." Tandy's words drew his attention. She was stacking the last of the china on the tray, her hands shaking and her gaze averted.

"Thank you." The words were gruff and hard.

Pearl looked up at him, her light brown eyes full of tears, and her lips drawn into a frown.

"Hey," he whispered, her expression softening his agitation. The world was scary enough without being frightened of your father. He knew the nightmare that was. He'd never be that man, never make his child cower in fear or cry from physical pain. *Dammit*. He forced a smile and wiped the tears from her soft cheeks. "No tears, baby girl."

Pearl blinked, her instant smile unnerving him. She shouldn't smile at him like that, like she trusted him. Like she could rely on him.

Tandy all but ran from the room, that tray rattling with broken china. Try as he might, he couldn't stop his gaze from trailing after her. But he stood his ground, bouncing his daughter in his arm.

"Click." Scarlett was all smiles, transfixed by the temptation of his baby daughter. Pearl had some sort of magical power, attracting women and making even the meanest sons of bitches smile. "When did you get here? Where'd you come from? A baby? Wow."

He glanced at his watch, deciding now was not the time to open the door on questions. He answered one. "Ten minutes ago. Hate that we missed the funeral." Traveling with a baby was no picnic. Not that he blamed her. Being strapped into that car seat looked pretty damn uncomfortable. Truth is, they'd sat in the truck through the funeral. He followed the procession to the cemetery but hadn't been able to get out of the car. Men didn't cry in public. He was confident Lynnie would understand.

He'd driven his trailer to the back of Lynnie's place and unloaded the horses into the far pasture—doing it all so he could delay *this*. "Pearl…" He broke off and shrugged, hoping that would be all the explanation needed.

He was worn out, emotionally and physically. The house was too crowded, the people too loud and curious. After he fed and changed Pearl, he wanted peace and quiet, a shower, a beer and a soft bed. If he was lucky, he could forget the mess his life was.

Chapter Two

Tandy washed every dish in Lynnie's kitchen. She cleaned out the refrigerator and swept and mopped the floor. She was hiding. She knew it and she didn't care. Until her cousins were ready to go, this was where she would stay. Cleaning was how she processed.

And dammit, she had so much to process.

She'd known seeing Click would be hard. But their past had nothing to do with losing Lynnie. And then… Today had been beyond expectation. He…he was a father.

Fourteen months.

If her heart hadn't already been shredded, this would have done it.

She'd told him to move on. And he had.

Wasted no time.

Fourteen months. Their time together hadn't been as special as she'd thought—to him anyway. He'd waited, what, weeks? That baby was evidence of that. She'd been catatonic, consumed by sadness. And guilt—guilt that chipped away what was left of her heart.

He'd been in bed with someone—

She couldn't think about it, couldn't stand it. It hurt. Deep, raw and angry.

"You're exhausting," Renata said, having planted herself on a kitchen stool seconds before.

Tandy smiled, rinsing out the sponge.

"I say we go get drunk," Renata said. "It's the only option."

Tandy shot her a look. "How do you figure that?"

"My brain can't stop spinning. I can only imagine what's going through yours." Renata's blue eyes met hers.

She was pretty sure alcohol wasn't going to fix a thing. Still, she knew her heart wasn't the only one hurting right now. "Scarlett's okay with it?" she asked.

"She will be." Renata winked.

Tandy shook her head and carried the mop bucket out the back screen door, letting it slam behind her. Poor Scarlett—she'd have no say-so in their plans for the evening. But spending a night chatting with Uncle Woodrow and Aunt Evelyn wasn't Tandy's ideal way to unwind. She was too wound up. They'd only make it worse. Maybe a drink or two wasn't a bad idea. Anything to help her forget for a while.

Banshee jumped up from his place on the deck, pushing his massive head under her hand. She patted him, dumped the dirty water out and leaned against the railing, gasping for breath. The past was over and done with. She had no right to feel anything. None. So her anger was a shock. But she was. Really angry.

Worse, she hurt.

I'm done hurting over the past.

Banshee head-butted her hand, groaning in the back of his throat. She rubbed behind his ear, his silky fur calming her. A little.

Fourteen months? Fourteen months. She couldn't wrap her head around it. Didn't want to.

"Is that Tandy Boone?"

Tandy jumped, spinning on her heel. "Brody?" She pressed a hand to her chest. "I didn't know you were here.

Last I heard, you were wheeling and dealing in Dallas, or something."

"Just got here. Nothing like a funeral to get people together again." Brody Wallace's hug was warm. "I make the trip once a month, or when Dad needs me. He's never fully recovered from his stroke last fall. Not that he'd admit it or say I was anything other than a nuisance."

"You're being a good son to check in on him so regularly. No thoughts of taking over the family businesses yet?" she asked.

"Soon, maybe." Brody smiled. "I came to pay my respects. Lynnie Hale was a rare breed."

Tandy nodded. "She was that."

"What brings you back to Fort Kyle?" Brody's brown eyes did a quick head-to-toe. "Not that I'm not glad to see you and all. Who is this?" he asked, nodding at Banshee.

"Banshee, my best friend, of course. We moved for a new job at the veterinary clinic." She squinted into the setting sun, the fence between Lynnie's and Uncle Woodrow's property visible. And just beyond the fence line sat one of Uncle Woodrow's hunting cabins. Wildflowers carpeted the space between, vibrant pinks and reds and blues a stark contrast to the rugged beauty of West Texas. Nothing like the rolling hills she'd left behind in Stonewall Crossing. *Please God, don't let this move be a mistake.*

"So you'll be around for a while?" he asked.

She shrugged, everything she'd known a few hours ago no longer certain. The job here paid ridiculously well, and she still needed some distance from all the weddings and babies in Stonewall Crossing. She was happy for her family and loved them dearly, but it was *hard*. "We'll see." She rubbed on Banshee then, smiling into his golden eyes.

"What's taking so long? You better not be scrubbing the porch or sweeping the rafters—" Renata's eyes went round when she spied Brody. "Brody Wallace, what are you doing out here?"

Brody laughed. "Enjoying the view." He caught Renata in a big hug. "Damn good to see you, Renata."

"You, too." Renata clapped his shoulders. "You should come with us tonight. We can catch up."

Brody looked back and forth between them. "Where are you going?"

"The Tumbleweed," Renata said. "Drinks are definitely in order."

Brody nodded. "I could use a drink. Any other Boones around?"

Tandy shook her head, knowing exactly what he was asking. "If you're asking if Uncle Woodrow is here, the answer is no. It's just me, Renata and Scarlett."

He winked. "He's not real fond of me. Guess it's the last name." As far as Tandy knew, the Wallace-Boone animosity began and ended with the current patriarchs.

"Is that why you're hanging around outside?" Tandy asked.

He shrugged. "No point adding more stress to the day."

"Agreed. We'll meet you there, around seven," Renata said, waving at him before tugging Tandy back into the kitchen. "No more. I'm guessing you're as ready to go as I am?"

Tandy nodded. "You get Scarlett, I'll get the truck."

Renata nodded, her blue eyes full of sympathy once more. "If it helps, he's in Lynnie's room with…with his daughter."

Tandy frowned, straightening. "I'm not hiding from him," she lied. If she was avoiding him it was because she was afraid she'd cause a scene. Not by yelling, that wasn't her style. But crying a river of tears was a sure-fire way to get people talking. Her cheeks were flaming as she headed from the kitchen to the front door.

"Tandy, there you are." Miss Francis gripped her arm. "We hoped you'd play Lynnie's favorite hymn for us. It was too quiet at the service today, what with Mr. Magee's arthritis making it hard for him to play. Seems wrong, don't you think? With her love of music and all."

She wanted to argue and get the hell out of there. But how could she? Miss Francis was right. She could do this—for Lynnie.

"Yes. Of course." With a glance at Scarlett and Renata, she made her way to the piano. She sat, running her finger along the newly polished surface before sliding the lid back. She took a deep breath, stretched her fingers and began. No one needed to tell her what Lynnie's favorite hymn was. Lynnie had hummed "What a Friend We Have in Jesus" all the time. She said prayer was really a long-distance call to Jesus, that he was always listening.

Tandy played, the straightforward notes and simple rhythm flowing from her without thought. She could almost hear Lynnie, knitting in her rocking chair, humming along. Voices joined in, filling the small parlor with song. She sang, too, the words long ago etched into her brain. By the time she was done, there were tears on her cheeks. Happy, thankful tears for the privilege of knowing such a strong and giving woman. Sorrow that such a life force was gone. And yet, she was one of the gifted few to know and love Lynnie Hale.

"That was perfect, darling girl," Miss Francis said, pulling her into a tight embrace before Tandy had managed to stand. "She loved to hear you play, loved that you loved music so."

Music was a comfort. Thanks to Lynnie, she'd mastered the piano, the guitar, the banjo and the dulcimer. Creating music and lyrics eased wounds and hurts too deep to ever fully heal. "She didn't give me much choice," Tandy said, wiping her cheeks. "I'm not sure I ever thanked her for that."

Beyond Miss Francis, Renata and Scarlett waited—crying and leaning on each other. Brody Wallace had come inside and had an arm around each of them.

And Click, stony and rigid, watched her from the door.

Black hair. Strong jaw. Tall and broad and muscled. Blue-green eyes that pierced her soul. Nothing had changed. Nothing. Except all the pleasure his presence used to stir was replaced with something jagged and sad and cold. She tore her gaze from his, sheer determination the only thing that kept her from breaking down right there in the middle of Lynnie's formal parlor.

"I'd say that was the perfect way to end the day. We'd best get," Widow Riley said. "You need anything, Click? With your baby girl and all?"

The need to leave quadrupled. She didn't want to think about Click and his baby girl. She couldn't. It hurt too much.

"Yeah, Click," Brody joined in. "We're going into town, to the Tumbleweed, if you want to join us?"

Tandy wanted to sink through the floorboards at her feet.

Scarlett and Renata stared at her, their expressions revealing the horror and dread bouncing around in her stomach.

"He can't go gallivanting." Widow Riley's disapproval was clear. "He's a father. I'm sure Pearl's mama wouldn't approve."

With a wave, Tandy was out the front door, almost

tripping on the wooden steps in her haste to get away. "Banshee, load up," she called out. Banshee came trotting around the porch, racing her to the truck and jumping into the truck bed and his waiting kennel.

Maybe she was overreacting. Okay, she *was* overreacting. Still, she didn't want to hear what was next. She didn't want to know about Click's wife, his marriage, his perfect family life. If she was lucky, he'd sell Lynnie's place and leave soon enough and she'd never have to see or hear the name Click Hale again. She hadn't been lucky in a real long time.

"I take it you're ready?" Renata asked, jogging to catch up.

She glared at her cousin, climbing into her truck and turning on the air-conditioning. "Scarlett coming?"

Renata nodded. "You sort of sprinted out of there."

Tandy's grip tightened on the steering wheel. "He's not coming, is he?" she managed.

"I don't think so." Renata's hand gripped her forearm, squeezing gently. "I know things fell apart between you, but I'd like to think he's still a little decent?"

Tandy rested her forehead on the steering wheel. "He… was." But seeing his daughter made her pause. Fourteen months. What did that say about him? The sting of tears infuriated her. She'd been lost in anguish and guilt so heavy it had almost crushed her. He'd started a family.

More important, what did that say about the love he'd claimed to feel for her? She had yet to date, let alone think about being intimate with another man. If he'd really loved her the way he said he did, how could he? No matter what she said and did, the grief was there every second of every day—a gnawing, aching pain. How could he replace her? How could he replace their…their daughter so easily?

It hurt to breathe.

"You sure you guys want to do this?" Scarlett asked, pulling the truck door closed behind her.

"Yes," Tandy said, throwing the truck in gear. She no longer doubted the logic behind Renata's reasoning. "Absolutely sure." A couple of shots were the only way she'd get any sleep tonight.

CLICK STOOD, STARING down the dirt road. The stone house was quiet now, too quiet. Only Brody and Miss Francis were left. And, suddenly, Click was in no hurry to see them go.

"What the hell was that about?" Brody asked. "You and Tandy?"

"How much time do you have?" Click asked, only partly teasing. He liked Brody Wallace well enough. Not that they'd spent a lot of time together—Brody's parents worried about Click being a bad influence on their only son.

"Sure it's hard on her," Miss Francis said. "Poor thing is her age, without a man or child to care for. And then you show up, with a sweet little angel to boot." She smiled at Pearl. "Can I?" she asked, holding out her hands.

Pearl didn't object, so he didn't either. After holding her for hours, it felt odd to have empty arms.

"First love is always the hardest to get over," Miss Francis said, bouncing Pearl on her hip. "If I recall correctly, you two had it bad."

Click didn't correct the older woman. But he knew the truth. Tandy wasn't jealous, she was disgusted. She couldn't stand to be in his presence. She'd made that perfectly clear two years ago, so broken and withdrawn in that damn hospital bed. And now this—Pearl—so soon after... He could barely look himself in the eye.

Miss Francis was right about recovering, though. He'd met Tandy over twenty years ago, and she still made his heart skip a beat.

"When will Pearl's mama be joining you?" Miss Francis asked.

"She won't," Click was quick to answer.

Georgia wouldn't be visiting for some time. The drug treatment facility she'd signed herself into lasted a minimum of sixty days. He was proud of her for getting the help she desperately needed, but he was devastated that it had taken her so long to get it. Not that he'd known. He'd left Tandy in the hospital and headed to a bar. That drunken weekend with Georgia was a blur of alcohol and grief. He'd been out of his mind and broken. They'd parted ways at weekend's end, and he hadn't heard or seen her since. Until a week ago. Her phone call had changed his life.

"So you're in this on your own?" Brody piped up.

Click sighed. "Yep."

"This a new development?" Miss Francis asked. "Don't get your tail feathers ruffled when I say this, but you look a little green when it comes to caretaking this baby."

"That I am." Click nodded, smiling at his daughter. One of Pearl's little fingers worried the beadwork on Miss Francis's sweater. "I was bringing Pearl here, counting on Lynnie to show me what to do. But now…" He shook his head, staring around the house. After chastising him for having a child out of wedlock, Lynnie would have been over the moon about Pearl. She loved babies, loved children. It was one of the great injustices of life that he'd been born to people like his parents while a woman like Lynnie Hale was childless.

"Oh, Lynnie would eat her up," Miss Francis said,

smiling at Pearl. "She's the sweetest thing, Click. You're a lucky man."

He reminded himself of that regularly. Pearl was healthy. Considering Georgia's drug problem, that was nothing short of a miracle. He had no way of knowing if she'd used through her pregnancy, no way of knowing what his daughter had been exposed to the first year of her life. He'd been hard-pressed to believe Pearl was his, but the DNA test had confirmed it, and Click stepped up. If he hadn't, his daughter would be in CPS custody.

"I'm going to miss your Gramma Lynnie, too," Miss Francis said to Pearl. "Who am I going to quilt with? Or go to ladies' meetings with? Or drive me into Alpine now and then to shop—I hate driving in traffic."

Click grinned. There was no traffic in Fort Kyle. There were four lights, around town square, and nothing else. Alpine wasn't much bigger. "I'll drive you."

Miss Francis smiled. "I'll take you up on that, Click."

"Guess I should be heading out," Brody said. "Not often I get a night out. Not that Fort Kyle's nightlife can compare to the Dallas scene."

"Enjoy it," Click said.

Brody held his hand out. "I'm glad you're back, Click, even if I'm sorry for the circumstances. It'll be nice to have someone male from this generation around when I visit."

Click shook his hand. "Thanks."

Miss Francis laughed. "S'pose Fort Kyle is more for those already settled."

Click looked at his daughter. He was settled now, as settled as he planned to get. He didn't know where he and Pearl would end up, but he'd make sure she had a roof over her head and food in her little stomach. It wasn't much, but it was more than he'd had growing up.

"Have fun," Click said.

"Be safe," Miss Francis joined in. "Roads get awful dark. Drinking's not going to help."

"Yes, ma'am," Brody said, tipping his hat her way, and leaving.

Pearl cooed, her gurgling noises a mystery to him. But she looked so damn cute, all big eyes, button nose and bubble-blowing lips, he was hard-pressed not to laugh.

"You got what you need?" Miss Francis asked. "Baby supplies?"

He shrugged. "Still figuring that out. Diapers, wipes, food, bottles, formula, car seat and a foldable bed."

"Clothing?" Miss Francis asked, her brow furrowing.

He nodded. "Enough."

"I have four children and thirteen grandchildren, Click Hale. If you need a thing, I'm a phone call away, you hear me?" Miss Francis asked. "How long have you had her?"

"A week."

Miss Francis stared at him. "A surprise?"

He nodded.

"You go take yourself a shower and a nap, if you want. Me and little miss here will do just fine." Miss Francis waved him away. "Or, if you're not tired, you go on and join Brody and the girls. Might do you some good to get out for a while."

Click almost argued. Almost. "I'll hit the shower." He nodded, heading toward the guest room he'd always stayed in when he visited Lynnie. It didn't feel right to stay in her room. He stood under the hot water and closed his eyes. He half expected her to bang on the bathroom door to remind him to get behind his ears—like she'd always done. Like he could get filthy behind his ears. He hadn't minded, though. It'd been nice to know someone cared if he was clean or not.

The last week he'd showered with the curtain and bathroom door wide open—in case Pearl had needed him. He was terrified she'd climb out of her bed or get out of their hotel room or pull something dangerous into her crib. None of which made sense since he went a little overboard baby-proofing wherever they went. He had one job, keeping her safe. The money he'd saved up on the rodeo circuit, first riding pickup then scouting stock, was enough to get by on for now. He planned on staying at Lynnie's place for a while, until he had to leave. He hoped he had some regrouping time before that happened.

He climbed out of the shower and dried off. He ran a hand over his tattoo, a barbed-wire band circling his upper left arm. Tandy's name was forever inked on his skin. With a sigh, he wrapped a towel around his waist and headed into his bedroom. But lying on the bed, staring at the spinning ceiling fan overhead, wasn't relaxing. His brain was too caught up in sifting through the events of the day.

He ran a hand through his wet hair and sat up.

He should stay put. Miss Francis was giving him time to sleep, without jumping up every time Pearl squeaked or fussed. If he lay there long enough, his mind would shut off and he'd get some sleep. That's what he should do.

He should not get up, drive his sorry ass into Fort Kyle and straight to the Tumbleweed. He should not make this day worse than it already was. She didn't want him there. Hell, she'd all but run from the house when Brody mentioned it. Going would do nothing but make him hurt worse.

He snorted, doubting that was possible. Besides, pain was part of his daily life. It reminded him he was alive and breathing. His mind wandered immediately to her.

Tandy.

The three seconds she'd looked at him... His heart had thumped in his chest, every nerve alive and firing. He swallowed, remembering every detail of her face. Eyes so deep and rich he'd happily drown in their hazel-green depths. Golden hair thick and soft, silk beneath the fingers, he knew. Her smile, for Pearl, had been so bright. That's what Tandy was—the light in his otherwise dark life.

Chapter Three

"Are you sure you don't want another one?" Renata was already waving down the bartender.

"I'm sure." Tandy covered Renata's hand with her own. "How many fingers am I holding up?" She held up four fingers and waited.

Renata frowned, her eyes narrowing then going wide. "Three? Four? I'm *so* not drunk."

Tandy gripped her cousin's arm to keep her from slipping off the bar stool. "Right."

"But this is the last one," their cousin Scarlett joined in, giggling. "Here's to a long-overdue cousin reunion."

It had been a long time since they'd been together. Since the summer between junior and senior year. Uncle Woodrow sent her home—so ashamed of her behavior she wondered if she'd ever be welcome at Fire Gorge again. Since then, life and distance got in the way. Renata lived in Stonewall Crossing with her father—Uncle Teddy—and her brothers. Scarlett called Fort Kyle home, helping her parents run their dude ranch: Fire Gorge. Unlike her cousins, Tandy wanted to stay as far away from her mother and her childhood home in Montana as possible.

"Too long." Tandy lifted her almost-empty beer bottle. "To cousins." Her bottle clinked against Scarlett's bottle and Renata's refilled shot glass. They might be cousins, but Tandy had always considered them more like sisters. And best friends.

"Looks like I'll have to move here, too," Renata said, downing her shot and slamming it against the bar.

Tandy winced. "I'm still considering this a trial run. No roots are being planted, not yet." Especially now that Click was in town. *Not thinking about Click.*

"Have you ever planted roots?" Scarlett asked, her large blue eyes clear. She had yet to finish her first beer.

Tandy shrugged. "Guess not. Not in ground *I'd* picked anyway."

"Here's to picking your own ground," Renata said, raising her empty shot glass. "Hey," she murmured, looking inside.

"You just drank it." Tandy nudged Scarlett. Renata had definitely exceeded her limit.

Scarlett nodded, giggling again. "Yep, good toast."

Renata smiled a wobbly smile.

"Now it's time to head out." Scarlett's giggles came from an even mix of amusement and worry. Amusement over Renata's state and worry over being caught, out so late and drinking.

Scarlett's father, Uncle Woodrow, tended to keep a ridiculously tight rein on his kids—on all of them—even if they were all grown. Unlike her beloved uncle Teddy, Woodrow Boone had always been an overbearing pain in the rear, and some things never changed.

Tandy was willing to overlook his control issues since he'd helped her get this job. A good-paying job, doing something she loved to do, in a place she had some of her very best memories in. Fort Kyle held a special place in her heart. Moving here to help Uncle Woodrow's buddy out at the local vet clinic was the best offer she'd received in a long time. And since Tandy had received her second thanks-but-no-thanks letter from the veterinary school in Stonewall Crossing, she took Uncle Woodrow's offer as a sign.

Until today. Today had made everything topsy-turvy in her head.

"Guess the drinking didn't help?" Scarlett asked, studying her.

Tandy sighed, smiling. "Sorry." Relaxing just wasn't in the cards for tonight.

Renata sniffed. "Maybe one more?"

Tandy shook her head. One more drink would give her a hangover—one more thing to deal with. Her sadness wasn't going anywhere. It pressed, cold and heavy, into her bones. Lynnie Hale was gone. Even though it had been years since she'd sat in the dear woman's kitchen, she was devastated. Lynnie had been more of a mother to her than the woman who had birthed her.

"It's getting late. Lynnie wouldn't approve of you being hungover because of her passing." Scarlett's attempt to guilt Renata into action failed.

They all knew the older woman would find it hilarious. Lynnie had had a wonderful sense of humor and a laugh that rolled over you like warm sunshine.

"You'd rather, what, go to bed? We're young…attractive… Let's live a little." Renata hiccuped, all rosy cheeked and adorable.

Tandy wasn't the only one hurting, but she didn't know how to make it better. Aside from Lynnie's passing, Renata was nursing a broken heart. Well, maybe not broken, but sore. She'd been dating rodeo emcee Mitchell Lee on and off for a few months now. He'd called the night before to tell her he wasn't going to be in town for a while so she was free to date whomever she wanted. Renata wasn't taking it well. Her six shots of tequila were proof of that.

"Fort Kyle isn't exactly a late-night hot spot." Tandy pointed around the dwindling crowd at the one and only bar in forty miles. The Tumbleweed sat right outside Fort Kyle's city limits. It wasn't officially a dry county, but the locals didn't approve of excessive social drinking. If you were out drinking late, everyone in town knew about it the next day.

Another reason Scarlett was probably getting nervous. "And we still have to drive back."

"Sing with me," Renata pleaded. "One song and we'll go." But her attempt to slide off the bar stool had her gripping the counter and swaying where she stood. "Or you two sing."

Scarlett said, watching Renata closely, "You need bed. And water. And probably some Tylenol."

"Tandy?" Renata asked. "Please?"

She was tired and her head was starting to hurt, but she considered it. "By myself?" The Tumbleweed's karaoke night had consisted of five singers, all of whom sang loudly and off-key. She couldn't do much worse.

"Sing 'Cowboy Take Me Away'? It's our song, remember?" Renata's smile wobbled.

Tandy and Scarlett exchanged a look. How could she forget?

"Then we can go?" Tandy asked.

"Then we can go." Renata nodded, a little too quickly—her hands gripping the bar to steady herself.

"I'm going to get you some water." Scarlett marched down the bar to the bartender.

"She's a little uptight," Renata mumbled. "You'll have to help with that."

Tandy winked at her, patting Renata's arm. Scarlett

could use a little more fun in her life. Maybe not six-shots-of-tequila fun, but fun. Hell, so could Tandy. Now that her late nights of studying and babysitting the newest crop of Boone nieces and nephews and cousins were behind her, she had a pretty clear social calendar.

"The room is spinning," Renata muttered, swaying where she stood.

"No, that would be the shots." Tandy steadied her. "I'm really sorry about Mitchell."

"His loss," Scarlett said, pressing a water glass into Renata's hand. "Drink."

Renata's nose wrinkled, but she took a long swallow.

"He's an idiot. You don't want to be saddled with an idiot for the rest of your life." Tandy grinned. "You have brothers for that."

Renata burst out laughing. "So many brothers."

Tandy nodded. She thought her twin brother, Toben, was a handful. Renata had a twin brother *and* three more to boot.

"Sorry we're late," Brody said. "My dad's nurse called, almost quit—again—so had to do an emergency intervention there. That woman is the only person he'll listen to. I'll bankrupt the ranch to keep her with us." He broke off, smiling. "What did we miss?"

Tandy was trying not to acknowledge that *we* included Click. Had he somehow misinterpreted her quick exit? Did he think seeing a woman sprinting away was some sort of hard-to-get routine? Her anger was back and warming her belly, mixing well with the two shots she'd knocked back sometime before.

Yes, her mad dash from Lynnie's wasn't the most mature way to handle things, but Click's daughter had been a surprise. Tandy had known *he'd* be here. As soon as Scarlett told them about Lynnie, she'd known he'd be here and she'd be forced to see him. It had been enough to make her consider driving back to Stonewall Crossing. But how the hell could she do that without stirring up suspicion? She couldn't. And besides, she wouldn't do that to Lynnie.

But now… Now, here he was, again, raining on their girls' night out. It might not have been all that good to start with, but he had no right to be here.

"I wasn't sure you'd make it," Scarlett said to Brody, casting a nervous glance between her and Click.

Tandy forced herself to keep breathing. She wouldn't think about today, his beautiful fourteen-month-old baby girl, or the urge to scream bubbling up in her throat. She'd try not to look at him, try not to hear the deep rumble of his voice.

"How's life, Scarlett?" There was that rumble.

Her hands clenched at her side.

"You know, nothing new ever happens around here. Not really. Family drama gets old after a while." Scarlett smiled, shrugged.

Tandy agreed. Uncle Woodrow and Aunt Evelyn had always been good at dramatics. She'd started visiting summer break after kindergarten. How many nights had she and her cousins sat on the stairs, listening to Woodrow and Evelyn carry on about who'd done them wrong this time. She'd been mesmerized at first. Evelyn was so pretty and Woodrow this big bear of a man. Their rants had lost their appeal when they'd started to nitpick and criticize her and her brother. Even then, Tandy admired how devoted the two were to one another. While the world might be against them—or so they claimed—they never turned on one another. Her mother had no one to vent to. Maybe that's why she'd ended up the way she was.

Click's soft chuckle made her stomach ache. Being here, in a bar, with Click—and her cousins—felt wrong. And right—familiar. She needed a way out. The only immediate exit plan was to sing.

Scarlett was talking. "I've missed you two so much. It's nice to all be together again, even heartsick as we all are. Lynnie would like that… Her little misses together."

"Stirring up trouble," Renata added.

"She would," Brody agreed.

Tandy did her best to act calm, all the while aware of every move Click made. It was infuriating—to be so damn responsive to the man. And not all the responses were bad. She knew better. Why had he come? From the corner of her eye, she saw his bright blue-green eyes sweep over her, saw his jaw clench before his gaze darted away.

Breathe in. Breathe out.

"Click? You there?" Renata asked, narrowing her eyes and peering at him. "Um, 's that you, Click?"

"It's me, Renata." One dark brow shot up. "How much have you had to drink?"

"Six shots." Scarlett wrinkled up her nose.

"Gonna feel that in the morning." Click took the hand Renata held out, steadying her when she would have slid to the floor. "Need a hand out to the truck?" His gaze caught Tandy's then bounced away, his jaw tight.

"No, no, no." Renata shook her head. "Can't yet. Tandy's gonna sing. She promised."

She'd do it, if she had to. But she was open to other alternatives. "Renata—"

"You promised, Tandy." Renata frowned at them both. "Stop being so…weird. It makes me sad, to see you two like this." Renata's blue eyes were full of tears. "Ya'll had to go and screw it up…when me and Scarlett had the perfect wedding planned."

Tandy had two options: anger or humor. Her anger was a little too unhinged, so that probably wasn't the best move. Once she started yelling, she might never be able to stop. Humor was the kinder choice, especially considering what they'd all been through today. So she took a long swig off her beer and laughed, letting her frustration bubble up and out. It helped—a little. "I'm sorry. I'm sure he is sorry, too." She glanced at him, regretting it the instant his gaze met hers.

"I might get married again," Brody offered. "Someday. You can plan my wedding."

Renata was all smiles then. "You mean that, Brody? You're the sweetest."

Tandy shot Brody a grateful look. "Time to get this over with." She shook her head and planted a kiss on Renata's cheek. "If you remember this tomorrow, you'd better be prepared to apologize," she whispered in Renata's ear.

"I won't." Renata gripped Tandy's shoulders. "You love to sing, Tandy. Always have. Go on, sing. For me." She swayed back, blinking. "Besides, we could all use some cheering up, couldn't we, Click?"

Tandy hadn't meant to look at him, but his expression caught her off guard. He looked so sad.

Click blew out a long, slow breath. "I could."

"See?" Renata's grin was wobbly again. "Go sing. Before I start crying again."

Tandy bit back her rising frustration.

"Can't stand to see a woman cry." Click's voice was rough, his jaw tightened again.

Tandy flinched, digging deep to lock up all the pain and anger he stirred. The guilt was harder to shut off—

but she managed. She could do this. She could make it through the next few days without losing it. She'd always been an expert at burying her feelings way down deep, thanks to her mother. Losing Click, losing their baby girl, had tested that—but she'd survived. That's what she'd been doing ever since: surviving.

CLICK STARED AT her, wishing he'd had time to prepare for this. For Tandy. Not that he was ever prepared for her. Something about her grabbed hold of him deep inside, waking him up, making him feel alive. Even when they were kids, she'd been an unexpected force—all acceptance and support, easy smiles and easier conversation. She'd been different. And important.

He remembered the morning they'd met down to the details. She'd been a little thing, a few years younger in age and spirit. Long braids, rips in the knees of both jeans, her soft voice lifted in song and four puppies trailing behind her. She'd been picking wildflowers to make necklaces for her cousins.

After one especially bad episode, his father had passed out drunk and his mother had driven all through the night to get Click to safety. She'd dumped him at the end of Lynnie's drive and sped off. He'd slept in the bushes, too sore and too tired to make it down Lynnie's long drive. He was black-and-blue, dirty and bleary-eyed. But Tandy had taken one look at him, smiled and offered him a puppy.

"She'll love you forever," Tandy had said, holding the black-and-white ball of fluff toward him. "Wanna go for a walk with me?"

From then on, Click was like those puppies, following Tandy wherever she went. He'd gladly follow her today, if she'd let him.

He slammed his beer bottle on the bar and swallowed down the old hurt choking him. He'd done this to himself, as always. He'd come here tonight expecting what? A third chance? To see something in Tandy's gaze that gave him hope?

"You okay?" Brody asked.

He nodded. "Tired." His gaze bounced from Scarlett to Renata, both watching Tandy as she made her way to the stage on the far side of the bar. Tandy's voice still haunted his dreams, soft and sultry, a husky vulnerability that demanded attention. This would be torture, wonderful, horrible torture.

"She good?" Brody asked.

"She's amazing," Scarlett said. "I'm not just saying that because she's my cousin either."

Brody chuckled.

Tandy took the stage, picking up a classic wooden six-string guitar. It looked more prop than instrument, but Tandy plucked and tuned until she was smiling. She shaded her hazel-green eyes and stared at the bar, smiling at Renata. "This is for the only momma I ever knew."

Click nodded, her words echoing his loss. Lynnie was that for him, as well.

Tandy's fingers plucked magic from those strings, the music filling the now-silent bar. When she opened her mouth, Click sat on the bar stool. Her voice, those words, left him spellbound.

Nobody sang "Cowboy Take Me Away" like Tandy. Nobody. The rasp of her voice drew every eye her way, pulled them in and left the audience mesmerized.

"Damn." Brody stared at him.

He nodded, swallowing back the sting in his eyes and the tightness in his throat. Tandy's voice was unexpected, in the best sense. When the chorus came, Scarlett and Renata joined in.

He smiled, unable to look away from Tandy. She sang, tossing her long hair and closing those eyes as the song came from inside her, for Lynnie. He felt it, the grief and love and gratitude blended together into something raw and beautiful. As she plucked out the last notes of the song, Click was on his feet, whistling loudly. He wasn't the only one. Her performance was impossible to ignore.

She bowed, placed the guitar back against the wall and crossed the stage.

"Let's go, Renata," Scarlett said. "Tandy sang your song. Now let's get you home."

"The boys just got here," Renata argued.

"Renata." Scarlett's whisper wasn't soft enough to miss. "Tandy's barely keeping it together."

Click's gaze searched out Tandy then. Because of him?

"Oops." Renata pushed off the bar then tipped forward.

Click caught her, swinging her up in his arms. "Gotcha."

Renata blinked. "Course you do." She frowned. "I'm not sure what you did to Tandy, Click Hale, but I'm mad at you."

Click nodded.

But Renata wasn't done. "How're we all supposed to grow old together? With you two hating each other."

Her words gutted him. Hate? Tandy hated him?

"Don't you know how special she is?" Renata asked, her voice rising.

He nodded again. He knew. Damn he knew. He woke up every morning knowing—regretting.

"Renata! Stop talking," Scarlett said, horrified. "Maybe you should let Brody carry her?"

"I can walk," Renata argued.

"Didn't work too well last time you tried," Click said. "Stay put. I'll get you to the truck."

"This way," Scarlett said, leading him from the bar. "Brody, can you send Tandy out? Let her know what's... up."

Click followed, doing his best to act like Renata hadn't wounded him. Not that Renata meant any harm. She was drunk, not thinking clearly. Still, there was a ring of truth to her words.

"I got the door." Scarlett held the truck door wide, stepping aside so he could deposit Renata on the back seat of the four-door truck.

As soon as he'd put her in the truck, Renata listed to the side, resting her head on a pile of suitcases.

He paused, stunned by the appearance of Banshee. He was in the truck bed, staring down at him, tail thumping. Click had given Tandy the dog when he was a puppy—their first baby she'd said. "Hey, Banshee," he said, holding his hand out. "Grew into those paws, I see."

Banshee groaned, leaning into Click's strong rub-down.

Scarlett slammed the door and stared up at him. "Click, don't listen to her. I've never seen her this drunk. She'll feel terrible, hurting you."

"I'm fine," he assured her, giving Banshee's head and neck a good rub.

"No, you're not." Scarlett shook her head. "I'm not going to chastise you but... I don't know what happened between you and Tandy either. Drunk or not, I agree with Renata on this. Neither one of you is okay, and it makes my heart hurt—for both of you."

Click shook his head, searching for the right thing to

say. "It'll get easier in time." Every day he woke up hoping that would be the case.

Scarlett squeezed his upper arm. "Glad you're back. Planning on staying for a while? Can I drop by and visit you and your new family?"

"Pearl and I would like that, Scarlett." He grinned, giving Banshee a final pat. "Not sure what's next, but you can stop by anytime." He headed back to the bar. The same time Tandy was headed out.

When she saw him, she paused—her posture going rigid and stiff.

Dammit. He kept on going, his heart picking up with every step he took. He'd made a mistake tonight, coming here. He wouldn't do it again. Should he tell her as much? Let her know he'd do his best to stay out of her way? Because seeing the effect he had on her dragged up all the self-loathing and shame he couldn't face right now. One good thing about being Pearl's father—it forced him to keep his shit together.

He tipped his hat as they passed, offering her some sort of greeting, and kept going. It was hard. Damn hard.

"Click." Her voice carried on the wind, bringing him to an abrupt stop. "I—I'm sorry about Lynnie," Tandy said. "She was a gift to us all."

He nodded his head but didn't turn. "You all going to be able to get home okay?"

"Yes."

He glanced back, knowing it was a mistake, knowing he'd regret it later. Later. Not now. She took his breath away.

"We'll be fine…thanks." She hesitated, her gaze finding his.

Damn if he wasn't caught, held tightly by his love for this woman. "Night, then," he murmured.

"Night," she repeated, heading toward the waiting truck.

He made his way inside, taking the beer Brody offered him and sitting at the bar.

"Something about the Boone women," Brody said, shaking his head. "Once they get under your skin, you can't get them out."

Click grinned. "I'll drink to that." Loving Tandy had been the greatest gift of his life, something he'd known he didn't deserve but couldn't bring himself to point out. It had been his greatest secret, one he'd protected for most of his youth. Hadn't she known she was better than him? He'd almost told her again and again. Until the summer she'd kissed him and he'd stopped caring. Seventeen and bold, fearless and desperate—that she'd felt the same had blown him away. That was the last summer Tandy had come to Fire Gorge. Uncle Woodrow had made sure of that.

"How's India?" Click asked. All the years he'd been carrying a torch for Tandy, Brody had been pining for Scarlett's sister, India. Not that Brody had ever acted on it. Or India Boone had the slightest idea.

Brody's laugh was startled. "Moved back not too long ago."

"That so?" Click stared at the man. "See her yet?"

He shook his head, taking a long swig off his beer.

"She still has no idea?" Click asked.

Brody's narrow-eyed look said it all. "*Nobody* does."

Click chuckled. "Can't decide if that's better or worse. Having her and losing her or…" He shook his head. "Never having her." He shrugged. "Cuts both ways I guess." As much as he regretted the loss and hurt they'd experienced, he couldn't regret the love they'd shared. In the short time Tandy had been his, he'd loved a lifetime. All the dreams and plans they'd shared were gone, but not forgotten.

Now he had something new to dream and plan for. He had Pearl. And his little girl deserved all the love and dreams and attention he could give her.

Chapter Four

"It's so good to see you." Aunt Evelyn leaned around the table to hug her awkwardly, again. "When Uncle Woodrow said you were coming, I cried."

"She did," Scarlett agreed.

Tandy smiled, taking a bite of her pancakes.

"I hated parting with you that way," Aunt Evelyn sniffed. "Hated not having you girls all together for the summertime."

Tandy kept her smile firmly in place. That summer had changed everything. She'd been sent home, embarrassed, because of her *inappropriate* relationship with Click Hale. If being sixteen and kissing a boy she was sweet on was inappropriate. Her mother had never let her forget how humiliated she was by Tandy's behavior. Or how lucky she was her uncle stopped things from getting out of control.

"Let it go, Evelyn," Uncle Woodrow snapped, patting her hand gruffly. "Tandy's grown up. She's got a good head on her shoulders now."

Tandy didn't let the *now* get to her. "Guess I'll drive into town today, meet Dr. Edwards and see the clinic."

Woodrow frowned. "It's Saturday. Closed up."

"Saturday and Sunday?" she asked, stunned. Weekends were emergencies only at the veterinarian hospital in Stonewall Crossing, but it was normally pretty busy.

"His nephew takes care of the boarders through the weekend. Don't see much point in you making the drive into town." Woodrow sat back, dropping his napkin across his plate.

"You'll have to stay in one of the hunting cabins for now," Woodrow continued. "They're still updating the wiring in the Garden Cottage. Hope to have it ready in a week or two."

"How was the funeral?" Aunt Evelyn asked.

"Good turnout," Scarlett said. "Brody came, but his father didn't."

Meaning her aunt and uncle hadn't come to the funeral because they didn't want to run into Mr. Wallace? Tandy took a sip of her coffee, eager for breakfast to be over.

"Lynnie Hale was an amazing woman," Aunt Evelyn said.

"She was stubborn," Uncle Woodrow mumbled.

Tandy bit back a grin then. She remembered how frustrated Woodrow got with Lynnie the few times his cows brought down her fences or when she'd let him water his cattle at her spring—on her terms.

"She had to be." Aunt Evelyn sipped her tea. "To hold her own with the men hereabouts."

Tandy agreed. From Scarlett's nod, so did she. She wished Renata was here. She made conversation seem easy. But Renata's hangover had other plans, like staying in a dark, silent room in bed.

"Breakfast was wonderful," Tandy said, ready to get the day started. "Guess I'll head out to the hunting cabin and start unpacking."

"Take her to the south field. Best shape," Uncle Woodrow said, not looking up from his coffee.

"When he says best shape, that's not saying much," Scarlett whispered.

Tandy laughed. "I'm sure it will be fine."

"Good, good." Uncle Woodrow nodded. "Dinner is at six, around the campfire. Booked solid, so join us."

"Thanks for the invite." Tandy smiled.

Both of her uncles ran successful guest ranches. Most of her summer holidays and school breaks were spent at one of the two places. She knew hard work was required to keep things successful. Uncle Teddy's Lodge was more a large-scale bed-and-breakfast. They offered low-key excursions like birding and wildlife walks, horseback rides, hayrides and the occasional campfire.

"Bring your guitar, too, Tandy. Nothing says cowboy like a serenade under a sky full of stars," Uncle Woodrow added. "Should be a clear night."

"Will do," Tandy agreed. For some reason, singing to strangers was always easier.

Unlike Uncle Teddy's Lodge, there was nothing low-key about Fire Gorge Dude Ranch. The large-scale ranch brought people from all over the world to experience the Wild West firsthand. They had over-the-top theme nights, a mock cattle drive, dances and overnight trail expeditions for those who really wanted to "rough it." The last few years, Uncle Woodrow added upscale dining, yoga and fitness classes, and a spa for those "city folk willing to spend big money for mud baths and fancy food." It seemed to be working—business was definitely booming.

Tandy suspected the dude ranch existed mostly to keep Evelyn happy. Her aunt loved talking and meeting new people. Her uncle hated travel almost as much as he hated strangers and lengthy conversations. The fact that the dude ranch kept his wife happy and brought in a pretty penny was a bonus her uncle surely appreciated. But their real wealth came from the oil they'd discovered some years back. That and the cattle Uncle Woodrow kept.

"If you need a thing, you let me know," Aunt Evelyn said.

"I'm sure it will suit just fine." Tandy smiled.

Scarlett trailed behind her from the dining room, speaking only once they were out of earshot. "Something's up."

"I sort of got that," Tandy said. "As long as I have four walls, running water and some electricity, Banshee and I will be fine."

"That might be all you have." Scarlett shook her head. "That cabin is in rough shape."

Thirty minutes later, she, Scarlett and a bleary-eyed Renata bounced down the rutted dirt road to her new home. Tandy's enthusiasm nosedived. The cabin was one room—and in need of substantial TLC. But the bed was big and comfy and there were large windows in three of the four walls. The fourth wall was the kitchen, a collection of burnt-orange appliances and curling wallpaper. A pop-up table was built into the wall, collapsing flat when not in use. Two wooden chairs hung on pegs from the wall to prevent overcluttering the space. To say furniture was minimal was an understatement. The only additional piece was a large recliner. She could function with her closet-sized bathroom. At least there was a teeny-tiny shower stall, a toilet and a sink that dripped. None of that was the problem.

What bothered her was the view.

This was the sad cabin she'd spied from Lynnie's back porch. Now, Lynnie's house occupied the majority of one window. Not just any window either. If she lay on her big comfy bed, *that* was her view.

"No curtains?" she asked Scarlett.

"We'll head into town and shop." Scarlett shook her head. "Might as well start a list."

"I'll stay here and hold down the bed," Renata offered, collapsing into the armchair.

Banshee sniffed his way around the perimeter of the room and sat, staring at her.

"Pass inspection?" she asked Banshee. "No rats? Or snakes?"

"Or armadillos," Scarlett added. "I hate armadillos."

Banshee's tail thumped.

"Doesn't look like it. Good news," Tandy said, rubbing her dog behind the ear and refusing to look out the window. Here she was, surrounded by an ocean of waving gold grass and wildflowers and rugged cliffs. Yet, just beyond the barbed-wire fence sat Lynnie's house. And Click's large gray truck.

"Lightbulbs," Renata said, pointing at the ceiling fan overhead. The light fixture was bare.

"And candles," Scarlett said, looking under the sink. "I'm thinking you'll lose power whenever a storm rolls through. Candles are cheaper than batteries."

Tandy grinned. Leave it to her ridiculously wealthy cousin to be cost-conscious. "Candles sound good. And matches." She opened the small wood-burning stove built into the far wall. "Wood, too, I guess."

"How about we bring in your gear and see what's missing," Renata said from the chair. "And when I say we, it's understood that I'm not moving from this chair."

Tandy laughed.

"Maybe you can bring in the bedding first?" she groaned, draping an arm across her eyes.

Scarlett giggled. "That'll teach you."

"Oh, I've learned my lesson, I promise," Renata

moaned. "No tequila. And no men. We should start a club."

Tandy shook her head. "I'm getting my stuff." She propped the front door open and headed for her truck, Banshee at her heels. "What do you think?" she asked him. "Lots of room to run. Peace and quiet—"

Banshee whimpered, staring at the fence line.

"What's wrong?" she asked, following his gaze.

The hot West Texas wind carried the distinct sound of crying to her. A baby crying. She slowed, glancing at Lynnie's house. Click was there, slowly making his way around Lynnie's porch with Pearl in his arms. He was bouncing her, almost dancing with her—but Pearl kept right on crying.

Banshee whimpered again. He loved kids—loved them. Tandy had taken him to every babysitting gig she'd had, so it was a natural development. Somehow the dog had determined that, since he lacked a herd to care for, his job was wrangling babies and children. And now there was a baby in need. The dog stared at her, golden eyes shimmering.

"Hate to point this out, but you're my dog," she said. But poor Pearl was wailing. Her dog wasn't the only one with a weakness for children. She sighed and gave up. "Go on."

Banshee took off, his tawny coat a flash in the tall grass, knocking wildflowers flat as he made a beeline for Pearl. Tandy waited. The minute Banshee reached Lynnie's porch, he barked and ran around Click's long legs. Pearl's wails came to an abrupt stop.

And Click laughed.

She swallowed hard and turned back to her truck, tugging her bag from the back with so much force, she wound up falling on her butt. She sat there, fighting laughter—and tears—taking slow calming breaths.

"What can I carry?" Scarlett asked. "You okay?"

She pushed off the ground. "I'm fine. A dork, but fine. Grab what you can." She grinned. "Bedding is in that suitcase."

Scarlett reached inside for the bag. "You sure you're going to be okay out here?"

"It's not so bad," Tandy said, inspecting the small cabin. Truth be told, it would be nice to have the space.

"I'm not talking about the cabin." She nodded at her neighbors. "What if he stays?"

Tandy shook her head, impersonating her uncle Woodrow as she said, "Let's not put the cart in front of the horse."

"I can't believe you just said that," Renata said from her spot, leaning against the door frame.

"It was scary good," Scarlett agreed.

Tandy smiled, hooking her backpack over one shoulder and lugging a large suitcase with the other. She'd lived too much of her life worrying over Click Hale. That was going to stop, now.

CLICK SHIFTED PEARL to his hip and unhooked the gate between Lynnie's and Woodrow Boone's properties. A gate he had put in years before. It was rusty after sitting so long, but a solid push had it swinging open. How many times had he and the girls met up after the moon was high? They'd been damn lucky never to have run into a rattlesnake or javelina—or any other trouble. Those were happy memories. When he came to Lynnie's, he'd pretend that this was his home and life was easy and carefree.

"Da-gee," Pearl said, reaching for Banshee and kicking her little legs.

"Doggie." Click nodded, repeating her words.

She smiled at him. "Da-gee. Do-gee. Da-gee."

He laughed. "You like that doggie?"

Banshee stopped, looked back at them and took off.

"He wants us to follow him," Click explained. He didn't know enough about babies to know if Pearl listened or not. Half the time he thought she understood everything he said. Others, not so much. Like when he was trying to rock her to sleep at 2:00 a.m.

"Da-gee?" she asked, leaning forward in his arms, searching for Banshee.

"He's over there," Click said, pointing. "Right there. Banshee," he called.

Banshee came trotting back.

"Da-gee!" Pearl squealed.

Banshee barked, making Pearl jump. Click smiled at her wide, startled eyes.

"Doggie said hi," he said. "Say hi, Pearl."

Clearly, his daughter wasn't sure she liked the barking part of the dog. Her little mouth was puckered. The excited kicking and hand waving had stalled out, too.

"Hi, doggie," he repeated, smiling. "Hi."

She looked at him. "Hee, da-gee."

Banshee barked.

"See, he likes it." Click nodded.

Pearl nodded. Whether she was agreeing with him or doing what he did, he wasn't sure. But she wasn't crying, so he was satisfied. How she'd react to leaving Banshee with Tandy was another matter. How something so little could make such a loud noise was beyond him. Pearl had champion lungs.

"Howdy," Scarlett said.

He nodded. "Banshee showed up. Didn't want Tandy worrying over him."

"I sent him," Tandy said, patting the dog on the back. "Sounded like Pearl needed some distracting. He loves kids."

Click couldn't have been more surprised. "You sent him?"

She glanced his way, barely. "He gets upset when he hears a baby cry."

"That makes two of us," he said.

Did she smile? A small smile, but a smile nonetheless.

He knelt, holding Pearl's hands while she found her footing. Banshee ran up, sniffing her up one way and down the other. Pearl thought this was hilarious—even when she ended up sitting in the grass.

"Banshee." Tandy's tone was soft. "Gentle."

Banshee looked at Tandy and sat, then resumed staring at Pearl.

"He's smart." Click was impressed.

"Da-gee," Pearl said, pushing herself back onto her feet and pointing at Banshee.

"He is," Tandy agreed, watching his daughter and the dog. "And he *loves* the attention."

Click's lungs emptied at the smile Tandy gave his daughter. Warm and real, sweet and carefree. The way Tandy should look.

"Since you're here, lend a gal a hand?" Scarlett asked. "It's heavy." She nodded at a large box in the back of the truck.

He nodded. "You moving out here?" he asked, inspecting the cabin with a critical eye. It leaned to the right, the whole damn building. Hell, a strong wind would probably knock it over. He pulled the box to the edge of the truck and lifted it onto his shoulder.

"Me? No," Scarlett said, hurrying into the cabin.

He hesitated. Pearl was following Banshee in a circle, but with his hands full, he couldn't carry her and the box.

"I'll keep an eye on her." Tandy's voice was soft, but her smile was gone.

He closed his eyes, wishing there was a way to ease the tension between them. "Thank you." He carried the box inside the cabin and placed it on the floor. Renata was sprawled across the bed, a towel folded over her eyes. Other than the even rise and fall of her chest, she wasn't moving.

"Recovering?" Click asked Scarlett.

"She's just trying to get out of work," Scarlett said.

Renata giggled. "It's working, isn't it?" Then she groaned.

He peered around the cabin. If the outside had been bad, the inside was worse. "Who's moving in?" He bit back the "and why" he wanted to add.

Renata sat up, the towel sliding from her face. "Tandy. You and Tandy are going to be neighbors."

"I'm pretty sure my dad is up to something," Scarlett said with a sigh. "I'm just not sure what. Yet."

He'd stopped listening after *You and Tandy are going to be neighbors.*

Lynnie's lawyer was headed out that evening, to go over the particulars of Lynnie's will. He didn't know how long he and Pearl had before they'd be back on the road, looking for a home base. He'd hoped they'd have longer than this—time to get sorted out. Having Tandy for a neighbor was bound to complicate that. "She's moving out here?" he asked, shifting so he could see out the open front door.

Tandy was kneeling next to his daughter, tickling Pearl's face with a flower. The sight took his breath away and turned him to stone. That, right there, was all he'd ever dreamed of. The two of them and the family they'd created. But his dreams were based on a different baby girl. Amelia. The baby girl who had kicked and rolled inside Tandy's belly, reminding them she was coming whether they were ready or not. They'd wanted her so bad…loved her so much. He'd held her once, blinking back the tears so he could etch every detail of her too-still features into his mind.

She'd been perfect—a mix of him and Tandy and pure love. Letting her go had been the hardest thing he'd ever done. Tandy's sobs still woke him, frantic to ease her.

But he couldn't make it better—for either of them. Their baby girl was gone.

He gripped the door frame until the grief subsided.

"Click?" Renata asked.

He ran a hand over his face, swiping away all traces of his heartache before they saw them. "Yeah?"

"You okay?" Scarlett asked.

He nodded. "Yep." He pushed off the door frame and headed outside. He smiled at Tandy and crouched by his daughter. "What'd you find, Pearl?"

Tandy was so caught up in his daughter, she forgot not to smile at him. "A feather. A flower. And this smooth rock." She offered the rock to Click.

Click took the smooth oval stone from her hand, ran his thumb across its surface—still warm from her touch.

"Rock?" he said to Pearl. "Rock."

Pearl grinned at him. "Da-gee?"

Banshee's tail thumped.

"I get the impression *he* understands?" Click asked.

"Rock," Tandy repeated, taking the stone from Click and pressing it into Pearl's hand. "Rock."

"Ra," Pearl said. "Ra."

Tandy clapped her hands. "Yes. Rock. Good job, Pearl." She stroked her cheek. "Rock."

Pearl clapped her hand, dropping the rock in the process.

Click bent forward for it, the same time Tandy did, and they ended up knocking heads hard. "Damn, Tandy, I'm sorry," he said, rubbing his head.

Tandy sat back, her hand pressed to her head. "Accident."

Pearl burst into tears. Banshee was up, climbing over Tandy to get to the baby. His tail slapped Tandy in the face—over and over. Tandy's laugh rang out as she leaned out of Banshee's tail radius. Pearl stopped crying, pushing herself into Tandy's lap and smiling up at her. She reached up with one tiny hand, stroking her cheek just as Tandy had done to her.

Click's heart throbbed, the tenderness on his baby's face the sweetest offering a person could receive.

Tandy's forehead furrowed as she clasped Pearl's hand in hers. Click heard her ragged breath, the slight hiccup in her laugh, and ached for her. Somehow, she managed to smile and press a kiss to each of Pearl's fingertips. And that smile, Tandy's smile, lit up the evening sky.

Chapter Five

The moment Pearl touched her cheek, Tandy was done for. Why that smiling baby girl picked her, Tandy couldn't fathom. There was no prompting or ulterior motive. Pearl wanted *her*. For the first time in so long, something cold and sad shifted to let the sunshine in. Maybe it was the way Pearl toddled after her on unsteady legs, reached for her with tiny fingers splayed, or hugged her calf whenever Tandy stood still. Whatever the cause, Tandy couldn't fight it. She didn't want to.

Even if it was taking her twice as long to unpack.

"I didn't mean to stay. Just wanted you to know where Banshee was," Click said from his place on the floor, wrench in hand. "Least the sink's not dripping."

"And you've kept Banshee occupied," she said, nodding at Banshee. Her dog lay at Click's side, his golden gaze tracking every move Pearl made.

"He was always herding little ones in Stonewall Crossing," Renata said, wiping out the kitchen cabinet.

"I guess I didn't think about that." Tandy glanced at her dog. "Hope he doesn't get too lonely out here."

"Shouldn't be a problem if he gets to visit Pearl every now and then," Scarlett said.

Tandy shook out the sheet, smoothing the fabric before stretching the elastic over the mattress corner. Banshee would like that. So would she. But if Pearl was staying, so was Click. "How long are you staying?" she asked, unable to stop the words from slipping out.

Click sighed. "As long as we can."

She risked a look his way. He was watching his daughter, a mix of pleasure and unease lining his forehead. She didn't know anything about his circumstances. Was he married? Where was Pearl's mother? *The woman he'd slept with days after leaving her in the hospital.* That jagged lump was back, lodged firmly in her throat.

"Between jobs?" Renata asked.

"You could say that." He shook his head.

"Ra, ra, ra," Pearl announced, toddling toward her father, dragging a plastic spatula behind her. "Ra?" she asked, holding up the cooking utensil.

Click ruffled Pearl's hair. "She's a little young to learn spatula, isn't she?"

Tandy laughed, she couldn't help it. And when she laughed, the others did, too. It was like they were waiting for her reaction and following her lead. Which was wrong. What he'd done was to her, not them. Click was their friend, a friend who needed help.

"How about *spoon*?" Tandy offered.

Click arched a dark brow. "That's some spoon."

She shook her head, her mood slipping when their eyes locked. He shouldn't be here. He shouldn't look at her like that—like it was okay to smile at her. She swallowed hard and turned toward the toddler still waiting for her new word. "Spoon, Pearl. It's a spoon." She spoke clearly, grinning at the way Pearl watched her lips.

Pearl grinned, dropped the spatula, clapped her hands and waited.

All four adults clapped their hands in answer.

Pearl giggled, running into Click's open arms. He

tossed her in the air, eliciting further peals of laughter. Banshee perked up, placing a paw on Click's arm.

"No?" Click asked the dog, setting Pearl on her feet.

Pearl squealed and ran across the room to Tandy, her little arms twining around her leg. Tandy was helpless to resist. She scooped Pearl up and tickled her, savoring her solid weight and sweet, clean smell. When Pearl yawned and burrowed close, Tandy cradled her close. "Who's a cuddle bunny?" she whispered.

"With you," Click said.

Tandy ignored him. She didn't want to be special to this baby. It would hurt too much when they left. She stared down at the toddler, noting Pearl's dimple, the bow shape of her little lips and the slight tilt of her nose. She was all peaches and cream, her eyes fringed with thick, dark lashes like her daddy. But instead of Click's blue-green gaze, Pearl's were a light brown.

When Click came to her side, she didn't know. But now that he was, Tandy was hard-pressed not to react. Angry or not, he still had a powerful effect on her. Until she learned how to change that, she'd do her best not to be too obvious about it.

"You want Daddy?" she asked, forcing the word out. "Daddy?"

Pearl stared at her.

Tandy glanced at him, pointing. "Daddy. This is your daddy, Pearl."

Click cleared his throat. "She doesn't know me. Not really. Not yet."

She stared up at him—she couldn't help it. "She doesn't?"

He glanced at her, then away.

"Daddy," she repeated to Pearl, reeling from Click's revelation.

Pearl looked at Click, then Tandy, then Click again.

"Da," she announced, loudly, her little legs kicking. "Da."

Tandy laughed, the little girl's pride irresistible.

"That's right, Pearl," Scarlett said. "Daddy."

"Da!" Pearl said again, smiling at Click.

Tandy turned, offering Pearl to Click. Click hugged his daughter close, "I'm your Da," he said, then set her on the floor. She toddled away, picking up her spatula and following Banshee to his spot under the window. She sat, then lay down, beside the dog. It was precious. She was precious. Tandy glanced at Click again.

The happiness on his face was right, and he should be happy—so why did it hurt so much? This wasn't about her. Whatever wounds they'd given each other in the past, Pearl wasn't a part of that.

And yet... Tandy couldn't forget. *Fourteen months.* It hurt.

"If they're not going to ask, I will," Renata said, sitting in the large recliner. "Why did you say she doesn't know you? You're her daddy, Click. All a person has to do is look at her to know that."

Leave it to Renata to speak her mind. Her cousin was right. Pearl was the image of her father. Same thick black hair. Same smile and dimple. Beautiful. Tandy focused on Pearl. It was easier—and safer.

"Renata." Scarlett was horrified. "That's downright nosy."

"Oh, come on." Renata rested her head on the chair back. "He mentioned it. Click knows I didn't mean anything by it. Right, Click?"

Click chuckled. "Right."

Tandy smoothed her quilt up, patting the pillows into

shape with a little extra force. "He has the right to some privacy. We all do."

Renata snorted. "Well, that's silly. When did we start keeping secrets? Ya'll know everything there is to know about me."

Scarlett stopped putting the dishes into the kitchen cabinet. "Same here. I know, it's sad."

Tandy hugged her. "It's not sad, Scarlett. You've got a good life."

"Doesn't feel like I've done much living," she murmured.

"What's that supposed to mean?" Tandy asked. She'd always envied the stability of her cousin's life. Scarlett's folks might be a pain in the rear, might be a little too invasive and outspoken, but they loved their children. Same with Renata. As far as Tandy was concerned, Uncle Teddy was the best father in the world. He loved and supported his children in a way Tandy could only dream about.

She and her brother, Toben, had grown up without a father, a fact their mother reminded them of every day. Susan Boone blamed them for his leaving, reminding them how lucky they were that she'd kept them. They'd grown up thinking she'd done them a favor raising them, even though she resented them every minute of every day. Tandy had done everything she could to show her mother they were thankful, to make her mother proud of her—but it was never enough.

"You've got a family that loves you," Tandy reminded Scarlett. "That's a lot in my book."

"I'd say you've done a lot of living," Click added. "Handling your uncle Woodrow and aunt Evelyn on a daily basis is no small accomplishment, Scarlett. Most would tuck tail and run." Click shook his head.

Scarlett laughed.

"Speaking of which." Renata yawned. "Aren't we supposed to go to dinner? Something about bonfires and singing and steak."

Tandy glanced at her watch. It was five thirty.

"Why don't you and Pearl join us?" Scarlett asked.

Tandy bit back a sigh. Of course Scarlett should invite them, it was the right thing to do. But, dammit, she wasn't ready to have him back in her life yet.

"Da-gee," Pearl whispered at Banshee.

Tandy smiled as Pearl reached out her small hand to pat Banshee's paw. Pearl would be oohed and aahed over, passed from lap to lap and adored by Uncle Woodrow's guests. She'd take care to keep as much distance between her and Click as possible, to keep the gossips from getting too excited.

"Your daddy's never thought too highly of me. Best not get him riled up in front of his guests." Click shook his head, scooping Pearl off the floor. "We should get. I'm expecting company shortly." He paused, looking at Tandy. "Hope we didn't overstay our welcome."

Tandy shook her head, trying not to get lost in his gaze.

"Da-gee?" Pearl asked, yawning.

"Night-night," Click said. "Doggie's going night-night."

Pearl's lower lip flipped. "Ni-ni?"

"Night-night." Click nodded.

Banshee looked up from where he lay on the floor. He did look ready for bed.

"Maybe he'll come visit us tomorrow," Click said, glancing her way. "He's welcome anytime. You are, too. All of you, course."

"If you change your mind, Click, bring Pearl," Scarlett

said. "Daddy's mellowed." She ignored Renata's laugh. "Besides, if there's one thing that turns my father into putty—it's a baby girl."

Click nodded. "I'll think about it." Pearl was playing with the buttons on his shirtfront as they headed out the door.

Banshee sat up, watching as Click carried Pearl back down the fence line to the gate he'd mentioned earlier. She rubbed Banshee behind the ear. "He'll get the hang of it," she said to her dog. "Until then, you might have to help him."

Banshee looked up at her, his tail wagging in agreement.

She shook her head and headed back inside.

"I'm worried about him," Scarlett said. "He's always been the serious sort but—"

"He's so sad," Renata sighed. "And you're sad." She stood, hugging Tandy close. "I can't stand it."

Scarlett joined in the hug. "Me neither."

Tandy hugged them back. "I'm sorry."

"Don't be sorry. Just tell us how to fix it." Renata's gaze searched hers.

"Renata's right, Tandy. You and Click have been dealt a raw deal your whole life. It's time to find the good— ya'll deserve it." Scarlett let go, stepping back. "I know you're not one for believing in signs, but maybe you and Click being here at the same time will give you—"

"A second chance," Renata filled in.

"No." Scarlett shook her head. "I was going to say a chance to make amends for whatever happened." She paused. "If you change your mind, decide you want to talk about it, we're here."

Renata nodded.

Talking about it wouldn't do any good, of that Tandy

was certain. She'd never confided in her cousins. Besides the time and distance between them, she and Click had cooked up some silly idea about getting her cousins and Lynnie together *after* the baby was born—a reunion and celebration. A way to introduce their new family to those who mattered most to them. Instead, she'd been too devastated to reach out, to share or talk about it with anyone. And her mother, so ashamed and disapproving of Click, said they'd never talk about it. It was over and done and nothing good ever came from talking.

There was no point in talking about it now.

But maybe Scarlett was right. She and Click had shared something no two people should have to go through. She blew out a slow breath. But assuming Click's sadness was about them seemed self-centered. "He's got a lot on his plate," she said. "Something tells me this is about his here and now, not what happened in the past." Pearl was pretty concrete evidence that he'd moved on.

"His here and now does seem all over the place," Renata agreed, sliding back into the recliner. "Why is my head still hurting?"

"Tequila," Tandy reminded her. "Let me find my pain reliever. You're going to need it for tonight." Uncle Woodrow was notoriously loud, even louder in a crowd.

"Yes, please," Renata agreed.

"I hope Click will join us tonight," Scarlett said, sweeping the wood-planked floor. "After his company leaves."

"Could be Pearl's mother," Renata suggested. "Is he married?"

"I don't know," Scarlett said, glancing her way.

Tandy shrugged. She had no idea. After her mother had chased him out of her hospital room, she'd blocked every thought and memory of Click Hale from her mind.

She'd had to. What he'd done to survive the days, weeks and months since then was his business. Considering he'd fathered a child, he could be married. But he'd said Pearl didn't know him... Not the words of a man with a stable family life.

Tandy's gaze traveled out the window to Lynnie's house. Who was Click expecting? And, if it was a woman, would she have light brown eyes—like Pearl?

CLICK STARED AT the sheet of paper. One page, no addendums or stipulations. No notes or cover letter. Lynnie's will was as straightforward as she'd always been. And, in this moment, he'd never loved her more. She'd given him what he'd never dared to hope for: a home.

"Sign there." Kevin Glenn, Lynnie's lawyer, pointed at the tabbed line on the bottom of the paper. "She put in those oil well pumps a few years back, out of necessity. She didn't like them, but she couldn't bear to lose her land. And, since she couldn't see them, it was hard to argue with the checks rolling in each month."

Checks rolling in each month.

That was his, too. His and Pearl's. Fifteen hundred acres of property. A freshwater spring. A herd of Spanish goats, one donkey, two horses, a solid barn and a relatively new tractor. And six oil wells, bringing in more than he'd ever make working his ass off.

"You look a little green, Click." Kevin Glenn clapped him on the shoulder. "I'm taking it you're surprised?"

He nodded at the well-wrinkled man in the battered cowboy hat. "Yes, sir."

"You should know how proud of you she was." Mr. Glenn tipped his hat back on his head. "I know it tore her up to have no kids of her own. But that's how she thought of you. Her nephew, your pa, was a sad disappointment. You'll forgive me for saying so." He hesitated.

He nodded again. To call his father a sad disappointment was generous. What his father had done to him— to his mother—was unforgivable. But he didn't like to talk ill of the dead. Hell, he didn't like to think about his father. The man had taken too much from him when he was living. Now that he was gone, Click figured he had more important things to think about.

"After your folks died, she wrote this up and never wanted to change it." Kevin Glenn tapped the will with one gnarled finger. "She laughed some, knowing you'd have the people so quick to judge you come calling in the hopes you'd sell her little piece of heaven."

Click sat back then. "Sell?" he asked, still absorbing what was happening.

Mr. Glenn's brows rose. "Hell's bells, boy, this land is worth more than just money. To the Wallaces and the Boones, it's about victory. Those two have been nosing around this place since before you were born. Now that there's a chance they could get it, hold it over the other, you best be prepared for the squabbles and the offers to come rolling in."

"Right." He blew out a long, slow breath. Lynnie had brushed aside their offers, determined to hold on to her land—her only legacy. The fact that she wasn't too fond of Woodrow Boone or Vic Wallace might have something to do with it. To Lynnie, Woodrow Boone was a self-important ass and Vic Wallace an unforgiving curmudgeon. Other insults included money-grubbing, unappreciative and bullies. Click had no reason to believe otherwise.

He frowned. Last time he saw Woodrow Boone, the man had been holding a shotgun, scowling at him.

He'd never met Vic Wallace, not formally. He and Brody had been bawled out by the man for shooting rabbits without permission. Even after Brody had explained he was trying to protect his mother's garden from the varmints, Mr. Wallace had turned a cold eye on Click and blamed him for his son's reckless behavior. He'd been asked to leave and not come back.

Selling Lynnie's place seemed wrong—especially since he knew she didn't want either one of them to have her place. But staying here, being smack-dab in the middle of a feud, wasn't his idea of a peaceful existence either.

Lynnie had been his confidante. Then Tandy. Now he had no one. And no idea what to do. He studied the old man. "If you were in my shoes, what would you do?" Click asked the older man.

Kevin Glenn laughed. "I'd cool my jets and wait and see what the great and powerful Wallace and Boone were willing to throw your way. There's no rush here, son. This is yours, period. Once you sell, though, there's no going back."

Pearl's baby monitor crackled, the sound of her hiccups echoing in the kitchen.

"That right there is the only thing you need to focus on. That little thing don't care if you're living high on the hog or out of your truck. As long as she's got you to care for her, she's happy. You hold on to that, you'll always be doing the right thing." Mr. Glenn pushed himself from his chair. "I best be heading back before the missus gets fired up. I'm late for dinner, it'll be a month before I hear the end of it."

Click stood and walked the man to the door. "I appreciate you coming out here."

He nodded. "People have been making bets about

whether you or her cousin in El Paso was inheriting the place. Just so you know, once these papers are filed, everyone will know you're the proud owner of Lynnie Hale's ranch."

"How long should that take?" he asked.

"Depends on Berta Santos, the county clerk. If she's having a good day, before the end of the week. If she and her kids are fighting, could be a month." He winked. "Night."

"Night." Click nodded at the older man, watching him make his way from the porch to his mint-condition 1976 Chevrolet pickup truck. It was a damn fine piece of machinery. Sitting next to Click's truck, it was hard to miss just how sad a state his own truck was in. Rusted-out, mismatched doors, the liner of the cab falling down and radio that had next to no reception. But, most of the time, it got him from here to there.

For the first time in his life, he could buy a truck. Something new if he wanted to. Something with reliable air-conditioning and no short in the headlamp wiring. He ran a hand through his hair and shook his head. Lynnie Hale had been one of a kind. His great-aunt had always gone above and beyond for him. Many a time he'd wondered at it.

Nate Hale, Click's no-good son of a bitch father, had seen fit to visit only when he was dumping off Click, picking him up or looking for a handout. Lynnie had never batted an eye or turned the man out. Click hadn't had much of a male role model, but he'd had something better. He'd had Lynnie.

He stared up at the stars overhead. "I know you can hear me," he whispered. "I can't thank you enough."

He glanced at his watch, knowing Pearl would be hungry soon. And, if he hurried, they could still make the bonfire at Fire Gorge Ranch. Part of him was curious to see how Woodrow Boone would treat him, without knowing about his new inheritance. The other part of him didn't give a shit about Woodrow Boone.

The same couldn't be said for his niece.

"I don't expect her to love me," he said, still searching the night sky. "But, damn it'd help if I could get her to forgive me. And get her out of my heart."

He pushed off the porch railing and headed inside. Pearl was chattering away over the monitor, so he headed into the bedroom they were sharing. She stood, gripping the edge of the port-a-crib he'd set up for her. She was busy pressing buttons on the play gym that was strapped to the crib's side, happy as can be.

"You up, snuggle bunny?" he asked. He'd liked Tandy's endearment. Try as he might, the name *Pearl* didn't roll off the tongue. It felt too formal for this big-eyed, curly-headed baby girl.

She bounced, smiling and gurgling with enthusiasm. Her little hands let go of the crib to reach up for him.

"Hungry yet?" he asked, lifting her. "Bet you need a diaper."

She blew bubbles, clapping her hands. "Da-gee, da-gee."

Click smiled. "The doggie is with Tandy, Pearl."

"Da-gee?" Pearl repeated.

"Wanna go see the doggie?" he asked.

She clapped again. "Da-gee."

"Okay, you win." He carried her to his bed, assembling the necessary equipment for her diaper change. It was a work in progress. About a third of the time, the thing leaked. Other times, Pearl walked right out of them. But occasionally, he got it right. This nap time wasn't one of those times. Her little dress was soaked through.

"Sorry," he said, laying her on the bed. "Don't want to make them too tight."

She lifted her legs up, her hands grabbing her toes, all the while blowing bubbles.

"Guess that means you forgive me?" he asked, tickling her tummy.

Pearl squealed, her carefree laughter easing the constant worry placed on his shoulders a week before. They were doing fine. Better than fine.

He changed her diaper, adjusting it twice for good measure. When she was dry and in clean clothes, Pearl started scooting to the edge of the bed.

"Where you going?" he asked, watching her hold on to the blanket and swing her feet—looking for the floor.

"Ba-ba-fllllp," she announced, her feet touching the floor.

"You did it all right. Down," he said. "You got down."

She smiled up at him.

"You hungry?" he asked, heading toward the kitchen.

"Num-num-num," she said. "Num."

"We'll find you some num-nums." He smiled, washing his hands. "I just said num-nums, Pearl." He shook his head. "Guess I'm getting the hang of this baby-talk thing."

"Ga-bllp-la," she responded.

He frowned, having no idea what she was trying to tell him. "Or not."

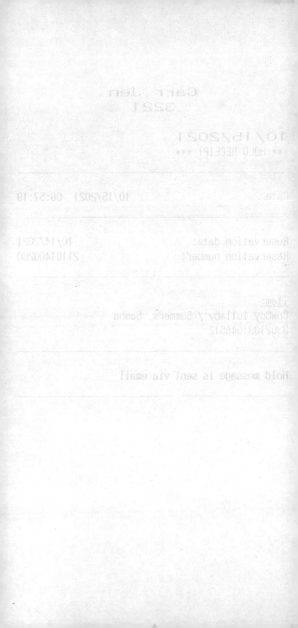

Carr, Jen
3221

10/15/2021
*** HOLD RECEIPT ***

Date   10/15/2021 08:57:19

Reservation date: 10/14/2021
Reservation number: 21101400200

Items:
Cowboy lullaby / Summers, Sasha
31021031048512

Hold message is sent via email

Carr Jen
3221

10/15/2021
*** HOLD RECEIPT ***

Date   10/15/2021 08:57:19

Reservation date: 10/14/2021
Reservation number: 21101400260

Item:
Cowboy lullaby / Summers, Sasha
33021031048512

Hold message is sent via email

Chapter Six

Tandy sat with the kids gathered round the campfire. They were red-eyed and worn out. That's what fresh air did to city kids. One of the things she loved most about the country was watching kids act like kids. Fire Gorge didn't get the best tower reception, so cell phone and television service was spotty at best. The kids normally recovered faster than the adults, chucking their phone for a dip in the pool or a trail ride. In time, parents were thrilled to see their kids playing in the dirt, climbing trees, running for no reason, skipping rocks and using their imagination.

But not all of them. There was always one parent—one family—that couldn't unplug. And for them, Fire Gorge was a missed opportunity.

"We're going to make some music," Tandy said, her guitar in her lap. "Anyone here play an instrument?"

One hand popped up. "I play recorder."

Tandy nodded. "Keep it up. Anyone else?"

Another hand rose. "I play violin."

The kid next to him tugged his arm down. "No, you don't. You don't practice anyway."

"The violin is a classic instrument. I know practicing isn't always fun, but it'll make you a better musician." She strummed her guitar. "We're going to go around the circle. I'll give you each a sound to make. We'll go around the circle, playing in order, and it will make a song."

"How's us making sounds going to make a song?" an older boy asked.

"Watch and see," she said.

He sighed, loudly.

Scarlett passed out the instruments: some tambourines, rhythm sticks, hand bells and shakers. She picked the older boy to play the bongos and a preteen girl sitting in the shadows for the spoons.

It was easy, really. She, Scarlett and Renata had done this countless times before—working through their summer vacation with the ranch's youngest visitors. Once the kids had settled down, she divvied up the parts.

Banshee looked at the instruments and trotted away from the fire pit. Tandy giggled. "He's not a music lover," she explained. "All my shakers, go first, like this." She shook her wrist twice.

"Then the rhythm sticks do this," Renata said, raking the long notched sticks up, down and back.

"Hand bells," Scarlett said, ringing the bell once.

When everyone had played their instrument a few times, they went in order, the sounds producing a steady rhythm.

"I'm going to play now. Don't stop doing what you're doing," Tandy said. She strummed her guitar a few times and started playing. "Sing with me if you know it. But don't stop playing."

"Let's sing a song and make some new friends…" she sang. "Follow my lead now, it's time to begin." She strummed her guitar. "My name is Tandy and I like guitar. That's something about me, now you tell me something about you…" She glanced at Scarlett.

"My name is Scarlett and I like to dance. That's something about me, now tell me something about you…"

Around the circle they went. Most of the younger kids joined in right away. She didn't let the older kids' rolled eyes or dismissive expressions get to her. That age was hard. But with each verse, more voices rang out. Someone started laughing, and that was all it took. The kids always got carried away with what they liked, but that was the point—to get everyone involved and happy. When they got to the last name, they were all singing loud and proud. They all clapped, laughing and using the instruments.

"Now that was some mighty fine tunes," Woodrow Boone said. "How about we take a break and have some burgers and hot dogs."

The kids jumped up, dropping the instruments and running toward the dining room. It was such a clear evening the windows and doors of the large hall were propped open. When dinner was over, the tables would be pushed against the walls for line-dancing and two-step lessons. She might have been expected to help out with lessons when she was a teenager, but there was no way she'd line up to have her toes crushed or her shins kicked tonight.

She packed up all the instruments and carried the large basket back toward the main house, staring up at the stars overhead. Texas skies were endless, always. But West Texas was different from the Hill Country. There, the rolling landscape offered a sort of gentle horizon. There was nothing gentle about the land here. It was barren and flat, except when it wasn't. The eye could trace the seamless line of the horizon then, boom, a craggy-faced cliff appeared.

The Davis Mountains weren't a vast mountain range when compared with their neighbors, the Chisos Moun-

tains of Big Bend National Park. But they held their own
beauty. Deep ravines, dramatic rock formations and an-
cient layers of vibrant volcanic reds painting their jagged faces. It was the minerals in the rock that gave Fire
Gorge its name. When the sun set, the sunlight reflected
and bounced, setting the rocks of the gorge aflame. It was
mesmerizing to see, the sort of beauty only nature could
manage. Humbling and awe inspiring, raw and soulful.

She paused, peering into the blue-black at the shad-
owy edges of the mountains in the distance. It had been
a while since Tandy had climbed up to watch it. Banshee, who came trotting to her side, would probably love
the hike.

"You know that was rude, right?" she said to the dog.
"You didn't want to hurt anyone's feelings, leaving that
way."

Banshee cocked his head to the side.

"Yeah, I guess you do have sensitive hearing." She
stooped, rubbing his silky-soft ear. His golden eyes
drooped as he leaned his head into her hand. "You're
forgiven."

"Tandy?" Renata called down from the porch, waving her inside. "We saved you a spot."

Tandy nodded, carrying the instrument basket up the
hill and into the main house and locking it in the equipment closet. Saturday nights were a big production. Uncle
Woodrow believed in sending guests off with a warm,
fuzzy feeling. The bar was open, the band was live and
the dance floor would be in use until the wee hours of
the morning.

She leaned against the doors and smiled down at Banshee. This was the first time they'd had quiet, just the two
of them, since they'd arrived in Fire Gorge. She knew
she'd miss Renata when she headed home. It would be

an adjustment, one of many she was making. But she'd be okay. She knew how to be alone—she had years of practice.

"What are you hiding from?" Click's voice startled her.

"Da-gee!" Pearl announced.

Tandy did her best not to tense. The past couldn't be undone, but she didn't want to live there anymore. If he was staying put, as he had every right to do, she had to get a grip. There had to be a way to see him without overreacting. Right now her emotions were all over the place: anger, sadness and…awareness. "Just enjoying the quiet," she confessed.

It was hard not to appreciate the picture he and his daughter presented. He wore a black button-up shirt, starched jeans, polished boots and a hat that sat just right on his brow. He was, without a doubt, a perfect example of a true cowboy.

Pearl was in his arms, waving at her.

"Tandy," Click said. "Tandy." He pointed.

Pearl looked at Click, then pointed at her again.

"Tandy." Click nodded.

Pearl grunted, leaning away from him—for her.

He frowned. "You mind?" he asked.

"Of course not," she said, taking the little girl. The scent of his cologne tickled her nose, threatening the dam she'd built against the tingle-inducing, molten-hot memories they'd made. "You look mighty pretty, Pearl." She ran a hand over her embroidered pink dress. "A little princess."

"Only one button," Click said. "I don't get why they use such tiny buttons on such tiny clothes. My fingers aren't made for it." He held his hands up.

Tandy laughed, too surprised by his tirade to do anything else.

Pearl laughed, too.

"Your daddy's doing fine, isn't he, Pearl? Tiny buttons or not." She should stop smiling at him, stop staring at him—stop drowning in those damn blue-green eyes staring right back at her. She sucked in a deep breath. It wasn't fair, this effect he had on her. "Taking Scarlett up on her dinner offer?"

He nodded, swallowing.

"Feeling brave," she murmured.

He shook his head. "Wish I was."

Her heart... It didn't hurt exactly, but it was feeling something. She didn't want to feel anything for Click, she couldn't. "Let's go," she said, too disoriented to do much but put space between them. The sound of his boots on the wooden floor, behind her, didn't do much to ease her nerves.

"Da-da-gee," Pearl said. "La-ba-gee." She ended with a gurgle.

"You want to dance?" she asked. "Well, you came to the right place, little Pearl."

"Is that what she said?" The amusement in Click's voice sent a shudder down her voice.

"She's dressed in a party dress," she said, refusing to look back at him. "Of course she expects to dance."

"You came." Scarlett jumped up. "Oh my, Pearl, look at you."

Pearl smiled, curling shyly into Tandy's chest. "Hee."

"You holding on to Tandy?" Scarlett asked, patting Pearl's back. "You always had a way with kids."

"And animals," Renata added, glancing at Banshee.

"Best judge of character," Click said. "Children and animals," he added.

Tandy stared at him, her heart *feeling* again…and thumping a little too fast. He'd stooped to scratch Banshee behind the ear, oblivious to how unsettled she was. Of course he was. It was a simple compliment, nothing more.

She turned back to the table to find Renata and Scarlett staring at him.

"Ta-dee," Pearl said, patting her chest.

She froze, staring down at the gleeful toddler.

"Ta-dee," she repeated, still gently patting her chest.

Tandy nodded. "Yes, snuggle bunny. That's right." She stared into those big brown eyes, Pearl's little nod of satisfaction filling her with happiness. "I'm Tandy."

"She said your name?" Click asked, standing close behind Tandy's shoulder. "Tandy?" His hand rested on her shoulder, warm and heavy.

"Ta-dee!" Pearl grinned, patting Tandy's chest. Then she pointed at Banshee. "Da-gee."

"Who's this, Pearl?" Tandy asked, looking at Click. "Daddy? Is that your daddy?"

Pearl nodded, her smile growing as she reached for Click. Click bent forward, his arms sliding under Tandy's to scoop Pearl up. His breath brushed her temple and ear. His hand, big and warm, covered hers. He invaded her space and her senses, simply by being there—shifting his daughter against his broad chest. Her hand was trapped, keeping her tangled up in him—them—far longer than she wanted to be. His chuckle was strained, drawing her eyes up to his. He was beautiful, as always. This close, it was impossible not to recall certain memories. The good ones. Like being in his arms. Click's embraces were solid, his arms strong and warm. She hadn't been warm in so long.

"As I live and breathe, Click Hale, don't tell me you're

still pining after my niece?" Her uncle's voice ended any
thoughts of warmth and being in Click's arms.

CLICK'S PLAN TO stay calm and collected just went to hell.
One touch from Tandy and control was a foreign concept.
One look into those hazel-green eyes and he didn't give
a shit about Woodrow Boone, his high-handedness, or
the man's ability to make him feel lower than dirt. He'd
rather stay this way, with Tandy against him, smiling
and flushed.

"Daddy." Scarlett's warning was useless.

Woodrow Boone had never made an effort to hide
how he felt about him. Click Hale would always be the
son of the man who caused the greatest scandal in the
history of Fort Kyle, Texas. Well, in this century at least.
Murder-suicides might not be all that newsworthy in big
cities, but there'd been no escaping it here. Especially
when loudmouthed opinionated pillars of the community made it clear he was just as bad his father—barring
him from having contact with his daughter and nieces
as a *precaution*. The comparison had sent Click into a
rage. He'd never raise a hand to someone he loved or let
his rage take a life.

He shifted Pearl to his hip, releasing Tandy. She
wasted no time putting a table between them. "Scarlett
invited us for dinner," he said, offering his hand to the
older man.

Standing face-to-face with the man who'd torn him
down when he'd needed kindness most wasn't easy. Time
had changed many things, but there was a part of Click
that still worried Woodrow Boone was right. Maybe there
was too much of his daddy in him to ever amount to
something good.

Woodrow's eyes went round at the sight of his daughter. "Us?"

"My daughter Pearl and I," Click said, forcing a smile. "She won't eat much."

Woodrow's gaze narrowed slightly. "And her momma?"

"Just the two of us," Click said.

"Hmm," Woodrow said, finally shaking his hand.

"Daddy." Scarlett hopped up and grabbed his arm. "This is Pearl. Pretty, pretty Pearl."

Pearl smiled her shy smile, staring up at Woodrow Boone with those big eyes. Click marveled at how quickly she stole the older man's starch. From inflated self-importance to grinning fool, Scarlett hadn't exaggerated when she'd said Pearl was the key to winning Woodrow Boone over.

Not that he needed to win the old man over—not anymore. At the same time, he didn't want to make enemies of his powerful neighbors. If he decided to stay.

"Pretty Pearl indeed," Woodrow said. "I see an angel in your arms, Click Hale. What did you do to deserve that?"

"Not a damn thing," he answered honestly. The last week had turned his life upside down and backward. But he wasn't sure it was a bad thing.

Woodrow nodded. "A man's only blessed if he has children to love him."

Click had never expected Woodrow Boone to say anything insightful, let alone true.

"Course, the love of a good woman's nothing to sneeze at," he added, winking at Click. "Where did you say the little missus was?"

Click shook his head. "I didn't." His personal business was his own. He'd decide when and what he'd share, not some nosy old man.

Woodrow's eyes went round, then he chuckled.

"Daddy," Scarlett interrupted. "That man is waving at you."

Woodrow frowned at his daughter, his gaze searching out the man. "Oh, well, that's one Jim Marshall of New York, one of our return guests. More money than a fellow has a right to. Best see to him." He glanced at Pearl again. "You and your pa come see me soon, Pretty Pearl. Might have a little business we can discuss."

Click bit back his smile. While it had never occurred to him that he'd inherit Lynnie's place, Woodrow Boone had probably been counting on it. He was curious to hear what Mr. Boone was willing to offer, but he wasn't ready to consider selling—not yet. Maybe never.

"Well, that wasn't too bad." Scarlett patted his arm. "Was it?"

He shook his head. "Not at all."

"That's the key," Renata said, patting the chair between her and Tandy. "Stay on his good side."

"I thought I was already on his bad side." He grinned, sitting. "Might be impossible to change that." As long as Woodrow Boone was civil, Click was content.

"Da-gee," Pearl said, giggling as Banshee sat his chin on Click's knee. "Hi."

Click shook his head. "Gettin' new words every day. Like a sponge."

"She is, so watch your language," Scarlett said. "We had a guest whose three-year-old ran around chanting one word over and over again." She shook her head, her cheeks bright red. "He had an older brother—quite a bit older."

Click grinned, curious. "What was he saying?" He was pretty sure Scarlett's idea of a bad word wasn't all that bad.

Scarlett shook her head.

Tandy laughed, leaning forward to whisper. "What did it rhyme with?"

Scarlett looked around, then leaned forward. "Luck."

He whistled, surprised. "You weren't kidding. Not the most age-appropriate word."

"Is there an appropriate bad word for a three-year-old?" Scarlett asked.

"No, not really. But maybe he should have started with a tame one. You know, something that rhymes with… ham," Renata said, laughing. "Or bell."

Tandy laughed. "Renata."

"Ta-dee," Pearl said, clapping her hands. "Hi."

Hearing Pearl singsong Tandy's name brought a smile to his lips. In the short amount of time they'd spent together, Tandy had made an impression on his baby girl. Click understood. Tandy did that, left an impression.

"Hi," Tandy said, reaching for Pearl's hand. "Hi, Pearl. Is the doggie taking care of you?"

Pearl smiled down at Banshee, her little fingers resting on the dog's head.

"Banshee is a good dog." Tandy nodded, rubbing the dog's ear. "He takes care of me, too."

Click sat back, amused by their conversation of sorts. Pearl gibber-jabbered, her face animated as she talked to Tandy. Tandy listened closely, her expressions just as animated, like she understood every word. Just when he thought Pearl had chattered herself out, she started again, drawing a huge smile from Tandy. There were other people at the table observing them, likely reading too much into things. But watching Pearl and Tandy was too charming to resist.

"Food's ready," Renata said. "Our table's up."

"I'll keep her," Tandy said, reaching for Pearl.

His daughter squealed gleefully, clapping her hands as Tandy lifted her high in the air.

"You're not eating?" he asked.

"Renata will get me something." She made a pouty face at Renata.

Renata giggled. "I will?"

"Please?" Tandy pressed her cheek against Pearl's, the two of them staring at Renata.

Renata sighed. "Shameless."

He liked Tandy like this, the way she'd been before. Playful. Smiling. Full of spirit and fun. Without sadness shadowing her eyes and twisting his gut. She was made for joy, not heartache. If there was something he could do to make her happy, he'd do it.

He followed Scarlett and Renata to the buffet line, reality returning with every step. He hadn't made Tandy happy in a long time. No, dammit, he'd been the one to put that sadness in her eyes.

"You still love her?" Renata asked.

He didn't say a word.

"Renata," Scarlett hissed.

Renata frowned. "I'm worried about my friends, Scarlett. Just like you. So don't shush me."

Click sighed. "No need to worry." Worry was pointless.

"Oh, really?" Renata asked, taking two plates. "She hasn't dated since you. Hasn't looked at a guy."

Click's throat felt tight. Tandy deserved love. He wanted that for her. And yet, even knowing it was wrong, Renata's words were a massive relief.

"What happened that made her so guarded? Why'd you guys chuck in the towel?" she asked, adding food to each plate. "Don't take this the wrong way, but you're not exactly the picture of happiness either."

He shot her a look.

"I love you guys," Renata said. "We love you guys. We've been too close too long to stand by and watch you two hurt like this."

"Not that we're wanting to pry," Scarlett interjected.

Renata sighed. "I'm fine with prying. Sometimes confronting things is the only way to fix it."

In this case, confronting things would lead to tears and pain. "Sometimes it's not," he offered.

They both stopped and looked at him.

"It would hurt all over again," he said, his words soft. He glanced across the room to their table. Tandy was up, walking awkwardly, holding Pearl's hand in hers. His daughter was following Banshee in a slow circle around their table. When Pearl let go of Tandy, Tandy trailed behind her—a smile on her beautiful face.

He'd learned to let go of the anger he had. Holding on to something hard and cold was wrong, especially when it came to Tandy. What happened was no one's fault.

"She's *still* hurting," Renata pushed.

"We both are." He tried, and failed, to keep the edge from his voice. "There's no way to fix it, Renata." He took his laden plate back to the table, shaking off his frustration when Pearl came squealing his way—arms outstretched—for him. He scooped her up, hugging her close. No matter what, he had this precious gift. Pearl loved him and he'd do his damnedest to make sure she always did.

Chapter Seven

"Polly sprained her ankle at the trail ride this morning. And Annette called in sick," Scarlett pleaded. "We're shorthanded for the dance lessons."

Tandy patted Pearl on the back, too smitten with the sleeping baby in her arms to care about her uncle's latest crisis. She'd done her duty, hosting the kids' sing-along and helping out with the marshmallows—and cleanup.

"Annette?" Renata asked. "The picture of health we saw at the grocery store this morning?"

Tandy nodded. Unless Annette had been struck with food poisoning, her illness was pretty hard to swallow. Again, not her problem.

Scarlett nodded. "You love dancing anyway, Renata."

Renata arched an eyebrow. "With men. That aren't married or teenagers or old and handsy."

Tandy giggled. "Old *and* handsy? All of them? Even that one?" She nodded to a rather distinguished-looking older gentleman, sitting stiffly in his chair.

"Especially that one," Renata agreed.

Tandy and her cousins burst out laughing. Pearl stirred, so Tandy went back to gently patting the baby's back—glancing Click's way. He was watching them, all smiles. It was the first time she'd seen him looking relaxed since he got here.

"Tandy?" Scarlett pleaded.

Click looked her way, his gaze probing hers. "I can take her if you need to help your uncle."

Tandy glared at him. "She's so peaceful. Moving her might wake her up."

His grin grew. "Might."

"I will if Tandy will. She remembers everything. I always just follow you two." Renata stood, stretching her arms over her head. "Stop hogging the baby and let's get the show on the road." She smiled sweetly.

Tandy frowned. "This is not fair. I'm busy."

Scarlett and Renata both smiled at the sleeping baby in her arms. But Renata recovered first.

"Click." Renata pointed at Pearl. "Take your child so Tandy can suffer with us."

Tandy glared at Renata, then Click. He couldn't possibly know how badly she wanted to get out of this. She was tired and emotionally drained. Holding Pearl soothed away the knots of the day, inside and out. Being groped and stepped on held about as much appeal as a hot poker to the eye.

Click held his hands up in surrender, his gaze shifting from Renata to her. His dimple appeared as his husky laugh bowled over her. There was a shift in the air, in her. Her irritation moments before was forgotten. Now there was only a molten throb deep inside. It was exciting to yearn like this. It had been *so* long. But it was also absolutely terrifying. It was always Click. He was beautiful. And tempting. And she was an idiot.

Time to learn from my mistakes.

Sitting there, holding his daughter, smiling and making small talk opened doors that needed to stay shut. She knew how real a threat he was. How easy it was to lose herself in him, to the sensations he stirred, and the strength of his arms. Something this fiery would only burn them both again.

Tandy stood, shifting Pearl into his arms as carefully as her shaking hands would allow. "Let's do this," she said, ignoring his startled expression and walking out onto the hardwood dance floor. "But you're taking lead, Scarlett."

Scarlett turned beet red, but she nodded, slipping the microphone around her neck. "Good evening, ya'll. How many of you are having a great time at Fire Gorge?"

There was a general rumble of approval, but part of the job was building up the crowd.

"I didn't hear anything," Scarlett said, glancing at Renata. "Did you?"

Renata shook her head.

"How about you, Tandy?"

Tandy shook her head, planting her hands on her hips.

"Let's try that again," Scarlett said, her voice wavering. "Who's having a good time here at Fire Gorge?"

That time, the crowd cut loose.

When the noise died down, she heard Pearl crying. Click was up, bouncing her in his arms as he paced back and forth behind the table. She fought the urge to offer help. It wasn't her place. He was Pearl's father. He'd calm her down.

But Pearl didn't want to be calmed down. Tandy held off through the line-dancing lesson, telling herself over and over Click could handle it.

Pearl's fretful "Ta-dee" was her undoing.

She crossed the dance floor, focusing on Pearl. Not Click. "Hey, hey, cuddle bunny. Hush now."

Pearl hiccuped, leaning toward her. "Ta-dee."

Tandy frowned. "Oh, Pearl. It's okay." She glanced at Click then.

"She wants you," he said, his voice soft and gruff, at a loss.

"I don't know why," Tandy mumbled.

"She's been through a lot in the last week." He moved closer, shifting Pearl from his arms to hers.

This week hadn't been what she'd signed up for either. But her thoughts shorted out when his hands brushed over hers. He smelled the same. Warmth rolled off him. And his hands, on her arms, sent a shudder down her spine. There was a sadness to him, a defeated quality, she'd never seen in Click Hale. She didn't like it. "Seems to me you both have," she whispered, pressing Pearl close.

His gaze met hers, guarded and wary. He nodded.

"Let's dance," she said, needing to break the tension between them. Now wasn't the time for conversation. Her uncle would undoubtedly be watching them like a hawk. And Pearl was still out of sorts. "She'd probably like it."

He nodded again, his gaze sweeping slowly over her face.

She carried Pearl back onto the floor, standing at the end of one of the lines. Click joined her, stepping into the stomps, spins and kicks with ease. As predicted, Pearl went from teary-eyed to wide-eyed, watching the smiling faces of the dancers around them. She giggled when Tandy dipped her, then spun them around. The dance steps were easy, most line dances were. By the second time through, people were catching on. By the time the dance was over, they were throwing in "Yee-haws" and whistles, and having a good time.

When the dancers clapped, Pearl clapped, too—and kept right on clapping.

By the time the next dance was over, half of Fire Gorge's guests were besotted with Pearl's huge brown eyes and bouncy black curls. She was pretty impossible to resist.

Whenever the music stopped, Pearl looked expectantly at Tandy. She bounced in Tandy's arms, humming and clapping.

"Dance," Tandy said. "You like dancing, Pearl?"

Pearl smiled, bouncing again.

"More?" Tandy asked. "Want to dance some more?"

Pearl nodded, looking around the dance floor.

So Tandy danced again and again, too delighted by Pearl's enthusiasm to care. When the line dancing was done, Pearl was looking heavy-lidded and drowsy. "Probably need a change before she dozes off," she said to Click. "Want me to take her?"

"Tandy, you don't have to." He glanced back and forth between her and Pearl.

"I know. I offered." She couldn't look at him for too long. Not because of the memories he stirred, but the longing. When her libido had woken up and taken notice, she wasn't entirely sure. For two years, she'd felt cold and hollow inside. Now, she was alive and...wanting. She brushed past him to the table, and grabbed Pearl's diaper bag.

Pearl didn't fuss as they made their way to the bathroom. She happily tugged off her slipper shoes while she lay on the changing table. She cooed and clapped through her diaper change, then reached for Tandy when she was clean and dressed.

"All better?" Tandy asked. "Nice and dry. Bye-bye, diaper." Tandy tossed the wet diaper into the bin and smiled at Pearl.

"Bye-bye." Pearl's eyes filled with tears. "Bye-bye?"

Tandy's heart broke. "No bye-bye." Tandy shook her head.

Pearl shook her head vigorously. "Ta-dee."

"I've got you." She nodded, forcing a smile as she

lifted her from the changing table and set her on her feet. "I'm here."

Pearl nodded. "Ta-dee."

"Let's wash our hands." Tandy set Pearl on the counter, pushing her far from the edge, and soaped up her hands. Pearl loved the water against her hands, so Tandy took her time with the process. When they were done, Tandy's shirtfront was wet, but Pearl was smiling from ear to ear.

Tandy held Pearl's hand as they made their way back into the buffet hall. Click was dancing with a teenager—a teenager who was doe-eyed and flushed with nerves. She knew how that felt. Click Hale was the sort of man who made women of all ages sit up and take notice.

Banshee greeted them, licking Pearl on the cheek and offering Tandy a short bark. Pearl barked back, making Banshee sit back and cock his head to the side.

"Pearl's saying hi, Banshee." Tandy squatted at Pearl's side. "Right, Pearl? Hi, doggie."

Pearl nodded. "Hi, hi, hi, da-gee." She toddled forward, wrapped her arms around Banshee's neck and pressed a big openmouthed kiss on the dog's cheek. Banshee, good dog that he was, sat still through it all. Then promptly licked her face.

"Ta-dee," Pearl squealed, tugging her hand and pointing at the dance floor.

"Dance?" Tandy asked. "You want to dance, Pearl?"

Pearl nodded, her black curls bouncing.

"Okay. Let's dance."

"SORRY IF I stepped on your toes," the girl said, blushing.

Click tipped his hat. "Not once. Besides, that's one of the reasons a cowboy wears boots."

She smiled and made her way back to her table, three

teenage girls staring at them, watching their friend closely.

"That was a lie, Click Hale," Evelyn Boone said, wearing a tolerant smile.

"I was taught to be a gentleman, Mrs. Boone," he responded. "Took a lot of nerve to ask me to dance. Didn't want to ding her confidence by telling her she broke a few of my toes."

Evelyn shook her head, glancing at the young girl. "Looks like you made her night." She paused. "So, Click, what have you been up to since last you were here?"

"Work." His attention wandered around the room, alarm bells ringing. Evelyn was looking for dirt on him. Did she think he was going to open up to her? She might never have insulted him to his face, caused a scene and humiliated him thoroughly, but she'd stood by when her husband had.

"You earn your living on the road, like your father?" she asked. "Driving trucks?"

Click swallowed, refusing to let her words get to him. She didn't know how he felt about his father, and he kept it buried deep down. "No, ma'am."

"I think Lynnie mentioned you rodeo'd a bit?" she asked. "Then you worked at the Sanchez place, training cutting horses, for a bit, too?"

"Yes, ma'am," he answered, knowing full well Lynnie hadn't shared this much information with Evelyn Boone. He'd never rodeo'd, too expensive for him. But he'd scouted stock for a couple of the rodeo companies. He had a good eye and enjoyed the work, travel and regular paycheck.

"And now? Are you still on the rodeo circuit or working for Mr. Sanchez?"

He grinned. "I've been training the last few years." The work made him happy.

His father had delivered horses to the Sanchez place a handful of times when Click had been stuck on the road with him. The first time he saw Mr. Sanchez working with horses, he'd known what he wanted to do with his life. From then on, Click begged to go back, watching the trainers at work and taking notes. When he got old enough, Mr. Sanchez offered him an apprenticeship. He hadn't earned a dime. But he'd had food in his stomach, a bed to sleep in and the opportunity to learn a skill he was fervent about.

He'd learned how key the team's connection was, finding the right partner for the horse and the rider. It was a damn personal thing. He took it seriously and, as a result, had earned a reputation as a quality trainer.

"Seems fitting, with your nickname and all. I remember you hanging out at the corrals in boots too big and a hat down over your ears, clicking at our horses. Always amazed me to see how they took to you, you being so little and all." She nodded.

He didn't mean to stare, but he'd never expected to hear flattery in any form from Evelyn Boone.

Her brows rose. "Well, I'm glad the Sanchez family is giving you work—"

"I've been on my own for a while, going from ranch to ranch and working with the horses and handlers." Being on the road had given him the freedom to work all over. Besides, he didn't have the facilities the Sanchez family had. Hell, he barely had a pot to piss in.

But now... He could do it right now, thanks to Lynnie. The idea blossomed, his mind already mapping how he'd set the place up. Possibly.

"Beautiful baby girl," she said, nodding at Pearl and Tandy on the dance floor.

He followed her gaze. Tandy was smiling, holding one of Pearl's hands as she rocked his daughter to the beat of the music. Pearl's giggle flooded Click with relief. His daughter was happy. Granted, she was in Tandy's arms…

He nodded. At times he wondered why he'd been given something so delicate and beautiful to care for. Hard work was in his blood. Dealing with challenges and risks had become second nature. But chasing after something so tiny, so fragile, made him downright nervous. Pearl had already slipped off the bed once, landing on her back instead of her feet. He'd held his breath as he scooped her up, terrified she was hurt.

"Ow," she'd announced, frowning.

"You okay?" he'd asked, running his hands over her back and arms.

She nodded. "Ow."

"Yes, ma'am, big ow." He'd stared into those big light brown eyes and taken a breath.

She'd smiled, clapped her hands and run off as soon as he'd put her on her two feet. So not as fragile as he thought—but not as sturdy as he was used to.

"Good to see a man smitten with his daughter," Evelyn said, placing her hand on his arm. "Shows he has a good heart."

He glanced at the woman. There was more to her words, there had to be. Unless this cordiality and interest was on her husband's behalf? Surely Woodrow had told her about his hope to buy Lynnie's land now that Lynnie was no longer around to fight for it. Damn, the whole town was probably waiting to see how this would play out. The Wallace-Boone feud had provided years of steady entertainment. Lynnie's land, who would get it, what they'd do with it, could be a game changer.

And this time, he was the one holding all the cards.

The music came to an end and Click made his escape, offering a murmured excuse and a tip of the hat as he made his way back to his table.

"Da da," Pearl said, smiling up at him.

"Hey, Pearl." He knelt on the floor beside her. "I saw you dancing with Tandy. You like dancing?"

She nodded, rocking back and forth, clapping her hands and giggling.

"That's right, dancing." He smiled, clapping his hands in time with her.

"Saw my mom sweet-talking you," Scarlett said from her seat at the table.

"She was?" Click arched a brow at Scarlett. "I thought she was just talking."

"Exactly," Scarlett said. "When has she ever *talked* to you before tonight?"

He shook his head. Point made. He was suspicious. Still, he'd like to think the past could be left in the past. Since he'd left Fire Gorge, his goal had been to make something of himself. If Woodrow Boone and Tandy's mother, Susan, objected because he was the no-count son of a drunkard truck driver and a woman with loose morals, he'd be better than that.

In time, he'd realized the only person he needed to prove himself to was himself. And he'd done that, for the most part. He'd lived life with enough sense to keep his head and keep his regrets at a minimum.

"Ta-dee," Pearl called, reaching out for Tandy.

Tandy sat on the ground, rubbing Banshee's back. She smiled as Pearl climbed into her lap. "What's up, cuddle bunny?" Tandy asked. Her gentle smile gripped Click's heart with fierce longing.

This is what he regretted. Tandy. He didn't regret how he dived in and lost himself in loving her. He didn't regret the time they'd had together, the plans they'd talked about or the vow he'd made to be hers forever. He regretted he'd let her go. That he hadn't fought harder. That even now, he could picture how good life could be for them.

"She was never nice about your mother. Or your father." Renata interrupted his thoughts, steering him back to Evelyn Boone and the flare of self-doubt these people still managed to stir. Dammit all.

"Guess I was hoping enough time had passed that people would stop looking at me and seeing my father." He hadn't meant to say the words out loud, not really.

Tandy's hazel-green eyes found his. "What they think doesn't matter. You know that. You've lived life without their approval. Don't let them change that now." She nodded at his daughter. "You've been blessed, Click."

His nod was stiff, the thrum of his heart accelerating at the intensity in her gaze. He'd spent hours learning how to read those green eyes. Hours of talking, hours of exploring, hours of loving. He'd known every light crease her smile caused, how expressive the sweep of her brow was, the mesmerizing flare of her hunger and pure bliss of her release. He'd seen the world in her eyes. And wanted that again.

Her gaze fell from his. "I should head out," Tandy said, offering him Pearl.

"You're really going to sleep out there?" Renata asked.

"That's the plan." Tandy's tone was tense—so was her posture.

"Since you've got Banshee watching over you, I think

I'll stay here with the reliable electricity and warm water." Renata grinned.

"I have warm water," Tandy argued. "Warmish."

"Ta-dee?" Pearl asked, smiling and waving.

"Tandy is going night-night," she said, waving back. "Is night-night right?" she asked, barely glancing at him.

"It works. Still figuring things out," he admitted. He didn't know what Georgia called things. Her note had provided him with the minimal instructions. Things like what words Pearl knew, her bedtime routine and her favorite toys weren't included.

Tandy was looking at him then. Eyes narrowed, brow furrowed. She had questions. If she asked, he might just answer them. One look told him she wouldn't. Her attempt to keep him at arm's length was being challenged by his daughter. Whatever courtesy or interest she was extending him was based on shared childhood memories and his precious daughter. Thinking anything else would only cause him heartache.

"It's getting late," he agreed, shifting Pearl to his hip. "We should head out, too. Walk you out?"

Tandy nodded, smiling her goodbyes at Scarlett and Renata.

The walk from the event hall to the gravel-covered parking lot was fairly quiet. Pearl hummed softly against his chest, her body relaxing against him. She'd be asleep before they made it home.

Tandy kept glancing his way. Every time, he waited, knowing she'd have at least a hundred questions for him. This resistance was new. Before, she'd speak her mind. But, unlike Renata, she was gentle about it. Tandy had always looked beyond the answers to the heart of the matter. She'd always done that with him—been careful with his heart. She'd known how battered and bruised it was.

When her gaze darted his way again, he said, "All you have to do is ask."

She sighed. "It's not my place, Click."

He stopped, looking at her. It took everything he had not to set her straight. Damn her stubbornness. No matter what had happened, she knew him best. How could she doubt that his feelings for her had changed? No, he didn't want people drilling him for information. But she was different, always would be. Whether he wished he could change it or not.

"Losing Lynnie's been…hard." He broke off. She knew how important Lynnie was to him, how healing the older woman had been to his spirits.

Her eyes shone with sympathy. They'd shared that, too, their love of his great-aunt.

Burdening her with the rest of his situation was wrong. He had no right to do that to her, knowing how big her heart was. This was his problem, his life, one she'd assured him she would never want to be a part of. Somehow the words slipped out anyway, "I don't know what the hell I'm doing."

Chapter Eight

Click Hale was a rock. She remembered the first time she'd met him. She'd been wandering through Lynnie's property, hiding from Uncle Woodrow and the constant chaos of the ranch. The barn dog's puppies had trailed after her, keeping her company. She'd been singing, loudly, when she'd stumbled upon a boy.

A beautiful boy with the biggest, saddest eyes she'd ever seen. The bruises said what he wouldn't. He'd stood there, defensive, glaring at her. But she understood immediately—he was alone and scared. And she had to fix it.

"I'm Tandy," she'd said, smiling her best smile.

"Click," he'd muttered, still braced.

"Click?"

"You know. How you talk to horses?" He'd demonstrated, clicking a few times.

She nodded. "I like it." She'd stuck her hand out, waiting for him to take it, then shook his with real enthusiasm. She'd offered him a puppy, hoping to chase away whatever monsters he was hiding from. Tandy had watched his wariness and anger slowly melt away. In its place was a smile that stole Tandy's heart.

Looking at Click Hale now, she saw the same damn thing.

Sure, he was proud, strong and capable. But he was

also terrified. And alone. Traces of the wounded boy were all too evident. And the hole where her heart should have been throbbed. It would be best to help him pack Pearl into his truck and drive away. She was barely managing on her own. Why put herself in a position that threatened that? Helping Click and Pearl was a risk. The sort of risk that could inevitably drag their history out into the open and tear her wounds wide.

He cleared his throat. "I'm figuring it out." But his words were a damn lie.

His attempt to reassure her chipped at the walls she'd built to keep him—hurt—out. It wasn't in her to turn her back on him. On anyone hurting. "Wanna go for a walk with me?" she managed.

He stared at her, the corners of his mouth turning up slowly. "I'd like that."

She nodded, glancing back at the ranch. "Maybe not here?" There was no sign of her aunt or uncle, but that didn't mean they weren't there. While she had a hard time believing they were still patrolling her love life, there was no doubt they were curious about what she and Click were up to. And Click Hale as a whole.

He nodded, glancing back with a shake of his head. "See you in a bit."

She followed Click's beat-up truck down the dirt road, bouncing through ruts and dodging a few cows that had wandered onto the roads. A roadrunner darted out into the beam of her headlamps. Tandy slammed on the breaks and Banshee leaned out the truck window, barking frantically. "You can find him tomorrow," she said, patting the dog's back.

Banshee sat back, as if he agreed with the idea.

They drove on, turning off on their drive and bouncing along the road. It was overgrown, left too long untended.

If her uncle was agreeable, she'd look into borrowing the tractor and the box blade to plane the surface. A bump or dip here or there was one thing, but this was ridiculous. And her truck shocks might last a bit longer.

Once she'd parked, she and Banshee made their way inside. Banshee sniffed around, always on alert. She appreciated that. Banshee was fearless when it came to protecting his herd. Anatolian shepherds were wired that way. What made Banshee such a good companion was his easy nature. Not all Anatolians were so accepting of new places and people.

"Nothing?" she asked when he sat at her feet, staring up at her.

He sniffed.

"Hungry?" she asked, opening the pantry. Banshee was a big dog, weighing in over 120 pounds and tall enough to put his paws on Click's shoulders when he stood on his back legs. His massive bag of food took up more than half of her small pantry. She balanced his large food bowl with one hand, carrying a pitcher of water in the other, and pushed through the back door. Once Banshee was settled, she paced the creaking wooden porch. Try as she might, she kept glancing at Lynnie's house.

Tonight would be the exception to the rule. She would not get tangled up in his problems. Or lose her head over Pearl. She had her own life now.

No matter what Woodrow had said, she was going by the clinic tomorrow. She'd rather have time to scope out her place of employment before the patients started arriving. From the few emails they'd exchanged, she knew Dr. Edwards also had a mobile unit he took out to the local ranches. If there was an animal within one hundred miles, Dr. Edwards was responsible for them. Another reason Tandy had been agreeable to the position.

She'd worked at the veterinary teaching hospital in Stonewall Crossing just long enough to discover how diverse the job could be. Her love of animals was ingrained. She'd been ten when she'd set up her own makeshift animal hospital in the deserted turkey shed at home. Her mother and aunts rarely ventured out on their Montana property, so she and her brother had spent most of their waking hours outdoors. Collecting animals, giving them all the love and affection she longed to shower on someone, eased her loneliness.

While at the veterinary hospital she'd dealt with emus, bobcats, dogs and cats, horses and cows, as well as a giraffe, a lion cub and several reptiles. She'd liked the fast pace, liked to stay busy, but was ready for the next step. And since her grades continued to put her on the wait list for admission into the veterinary school, she hadn't been sure what the next step was. Until the job offer in Fort Kyle came in. Starting over someplace familiar, being close to Lynnie and Scarlett, made the decision easy. Fort Kyle's clients might not be quite as varied, but her experience had prepared her for pretty much anything.

Well, in the workplace.

Life outside of work was still a challenge. She glanced at Lynnie's house again. *Obviously.*

Two years and three weeks had passed since… She couldn't think it. Couldn't go there. Because nothing had changed. Not on the inside. Every day she got out of bed, got dressed, went through the motions and fought back the crippling grief that threatened to drown her. It was like moving through cement, weighing her down, pressing in on her until breathing was a chore.

How could she let go? How could she move on? She'd lost her daughter that day. But she'd lost herself, as well.

Banshee sat up, staring off into the dark, his ears

perked up and his tail rigid. She stared into the darkness, the opposite direction of Lynnie's place. Banshee's keen senses were picking up on something her human eyes couldn't. Whatever it was, he was on high alert.

Her phone vibrated, making her jump. She pulled it from her pocket and looked down.

Got your number from Scarlett. Pearl's sleeping. Rain check on the walk?—Click

She stared at the text. This was good. This was right. So why wasn't she relieved?

Sure. She stared at the text, hit Send and shoved the phone back into her pocket. Her hands gripped the splintered porch railing.

Banshee was on his feet then, the hair along the back of his neck bristling and a low growl rumbling up from his chest.

"Let's call it a night," she said to Banshee, using her most cajoling voice. "Okay?"

He whimpered, glancing from her to the dark and back again.

"I know you could beat it, whatever it is." She ran a hand down his back then headed in the house. "Come on, Banshee," she called out to him.

He barked once, the need to defend his person and his territory overruling her. But once the warning was issued, he trotted into the house and flopped on the massive dog bed beneath the window.

"You're a good boy," she said, sliding the lock into place. She knew Banshee could protect her, no matter what. But he didn't spook easy. "We're getting up early tomorrow. Going to check out the clinic and explore a little of Fort Kyle."

Banshee rested his head on his paws, those golden eyes drooping shut. She could only hope sleep would find her so easily.

It was barely six in the morning. Click yawned, watching Pearl toddle across the living room. She was into everything. He'd already moved Lynnie's teacup collection up onto the highest shelf of her ornate bookcase. All the framed pictures, books and treasured knickknacks that reminded him of Lynnie had also been moved outside his inquisitive daughter's reach.

Now he was worried about her climbing up the carved bookcase. Or pinching her fingers in the door hinges.

He needed to check on the horses, assess the state of the barn and start making repairs. Whether he was selling or staying, the place needed some TLC. But how was he supposed to get anything done with Pearl underfoot?

Lynnie would have occupied her and told him what to do. If he sat still, he could almost hear her in the kitchen, or the creak of her rocker as she swayed slowly, knitting spilling from her lap and onto the floor. Her patience had been as boundless as her energy. He could use some of both right about now.

"Da da," Pearl said, smiling as she hurried across the floor to him. She held up his keys, jangling them. "Da da."

"Keys?" he said, smiling and lifting her into his lap. "You like making noise?" he asked, standing. "It does jingle."

She shook the keys.

"Yep, jingle." He eyed the coffeepot, steaming and spewing—but no coffee was filling the pot. Coffee was a necessity.

She nodded, shaking the keys vigorously.

"You like music?" he asked, remembering how much she'd enjoyed dancing last night. She'd hummed herself to sleep in her car seat. "Music," he said, walking to the radio Lynnie kept on the counter. He flipped it on, tuning it to one of the three stations. Classic country tunes, steel guitars and a fiddle, spilled out into the room. "Music."

Pearl stared at the little box, her eyes going round. "Mew…"

"Music," he repeated, fascinated by how quick she was. "Mu-sic."

"Mew-sik," she repeated.

He grinned, spinning her around. "Music. You're a smart little snuggle bunny, Pearl."

She rested her head on his shoulder, smiling her shy smile up at him.

"Pearl, you're smart and sweet and pretty," he said. If his childhood had taught him one thing, it was the importance of praise. One kind word could change his day. He'd make damn sure Pearl always heard them. "Hungry?" he asked. "Yum-yums?"

She nodded, dropping his keys to clap her little hands.

He pulled all the Tupperware dishes onto the floor and handed her a wooden spoon, letting her make as much noise as she wanted while he dug through the remaining jars of baby food. He read over Georgia's notes again, made the cereal with applesauce and placed Pearl in the high chair.

"Forgot." He jumped up, rifling through the bag for a bib.

Pearl stretched her neck up and he put the bib on.

Breakfast was a quiet affair. Pearl was a good eater, gobbling up her cereal then turning away when she'd had enough.

"Done?" he asked, wiping her face. "Done?"

She wrinkled her nose up.

He giggled, spooning up the runny cereal. "Yeah, I don't know how you eat this stuff."

She smiled then.

"We should head into town, get you some more food. And diapers. Might stop by Miss Francis's place, too, and see about getting some help for you. And me." He ran a washcloth under warm water and wiped her face clean. How bits of cereal ended up in her black curls, he wasn't sure. But he did the best he could to get it out.

"Do-gee," she said, leaning away from the washcloth. "Da-gee?"

"You want to see Banshee?" he asked.

She nodded. "Da-gee."

"We'll see," he said, not making any promises. "Let's go see Domino and Blackjack. Get the horses fed."

She clapped her hands.

He was glad she was interested in the horses, and not scared. And yet, she was awful little to be poking around the barn without constant supervision. The place had been untended for too long, critters could have taken up residence. His toddler didn't need to be the one to discover them.

It took the better part of an hour to get the horses fed and turned into the pasture behind the barn. He kept Pearl close, making it ten times harder than it should have been. His gaze wandered the fences, knowing he needed to ride along the entire property. If they were solid, he'd look into cordoning off a larger area for the horses to graze and roam. He had no idea how to do that with Pearl.

As he snapped her into her car seat, he glanced at Tandy's cabin. Her truck was gone, no sign of Banshee on the porch. He stopped and stared, peering at the tall, dry grass around Tandy's place. It was overgrown with cactus, Apache plume and wildflowers. The rains had been good so far, keeping the burn bans to a minimum. Still, she'd be wise to invest in some goats or sheep—it would keep Banshee occupied.

He doubted she'd want much advice from him.

The drive into town reminded him how much he loved this land. Exposed rock jutted up from the earth, layered and stark against the endless blues of the Texas sky. Each time he visited, he'd try to learn more about the place he considered his real home. Lynnie knew everything. About the volcanic eruption that formed Frazier Canyon, Sleeping Lion and Barrel Springs. Explaining that the arrowheads he'd find from time to time could be Apache, Comanche or Kiowa. She'd kept him busy for hours, hunting dinosaur bones or fossils. When he found something, she'd polish it up and place it on the mantel like a prize.

He glanced at Pearl in the rearview mirror, wanting her to have memories like that. Vivid and warm, magically transporting him to a place when things were easier. Life didn't have to be hard. He'd do his best to make sure it wasn't for his daughter.

He thought of Georgia then, resentment and frustration rising up. Her life had been anything but easy, he knew that. But she knew the difference between right and wrong. Keeping Pearl a secret from him was unforgivable. More so when he'd learned she'd tried to use Pearl to get herself a husband. Apparently her pick had more to offer her and Pearl than Click ever could. A safe and secure home, with no money worries or danger. But once the DNA test showed Pearl wasn't his, the man had left her, and Georgia's downward spiral had turned dangerous.

He was forever thankful for whatever instinct had prompted her phone call.

"Da da," Pearl called out. "Mew-sik."

He nodded. "Yes, ma'am." He turned on the radio, smiling as her hands and feet bounced along with the Dolly Parton song filling his truck cab. As they entered the small town, his gaze swept Main Street.

The same grand hotel stood across from what would have been the saloon, just as it had over a hundred years ago. But the saloon was now a soda shop, catering to tourists who traveled this far to visit the fort and observatory a few miles out of town. Fort Kyle was a pretty little town with an interesting history and just enough events and special happenings to make it worth the visit.

"Maybe we can get some ice cream," he said to Pearl.

Pearl waved at him in the rearview mirror, the offer of ice cream causing no further reaction.

"Too young for ice cream?" he asked. He hated not knowing. "Might have to see if we can find a book on… raising a toddler?"

She clapped her hands then, her feet bouncing.

"The library might just work," he said. "Might find you some books, too."

"Da da," she sang. "Da da da."

"I'll take that as a yes," he said, turning at the fork in the road and driving the short distance to the library. "Except it's closed on Sundays." He shook his head. If he remembered correctly, most things were closed on Sundays in Fort Kyle.

He sighed and leaned back.

Two shops down was Fort Kyle's veterinary clinic. Tandy's truck sat out front. That's why she was here—for a job. She had a life. He was undoubtedly a bump she'd rather avoid. He may have lain in bed thinking of all the things he wished he'd said and done differently when it came to Tandy Boone, but that didn't mean she had. He had a lot more to figure out than just parenting. He had to figure out how to coexist with Tandy without wanting the impossible.

He blew out a slow breath and put the truck in Reverse. "We'll come back for books. Let's go see what they have at the grocery store. Sounds good, Pearl?"

Pearl nodded, still singing. "Da-mew-gee." She paused. "Mew-sik, da-da-da-do-gee."

Click shook his head. "All right, then, sounds like a plan."

Chapter Nine

Tandy ran a hand over her face and slid the file back into the filing cabinet. Her first week working with James M. Edwards had been...exhausting. She'd predicted some hiccups, but this had surpassed her every expectation.

The man was deaf as a post, slower than a turtle, beyond rude and so old twice Tandy had thought he was dead, slumped over his desk. Charlene, the receptionist, had told her he needed at least two catnaps a day to keep his mind sharp. Tandy had had no answer for that.

But it was more than her employer. She'd stayed late every night this week, trying to make headway. The kennels were a mess. Dr. Edwards employed his two teenage grandsons to keep them up. They weren't. But chastising either one of them earned her snorts and eye rolls.

The technology... There wasn't much. Charlene had a desktop that looked older than Tandy. The two in the office—one for her and one for Dr. Edwards—weren't much better. She'd yet to see Dr. Edwards turn his on. There were no scanners, the printer clicked and groaned, and Charlene had left the fax machine off two of the five days they'd been open.

The filing system had almost sent Tandy packing. Apparently Dr. Edwards's system consisted of putting folders in the drawers with no rhyme or reason. She'd flipped through, searching alphabetically, by species, then—still hopeful—by appointment date. So far, nothing was gelling. Which made pulling patient records damn difficult. When she had managed to find one of the four files she'd been looking for, Dr. Edwards's abbreviations had been indecipherable.

When she'd asked what they meant, her patience had almost snapped.

"Dr. Edwards, can you tell me what these notes mean? This is for Frisky, Miss Francis's tabby. She's here for a checkup." She waited, hoping he'd offer some insight.

"Miss Francis's tabby?" He peered over the rim of his glasses and squinted. "Tabby, huh? She used to raise those damn fainting goats, she tell you that? Damndest thing to see. They get spooked and then fall over." He chuckled. "Course, it's not a highly useful trait when they have a run-in with a mountain lion, let me tell you." He shook his head.

She stared at him, befuddled by the way his mind wandered.

He stared back, a frown forming on his well-lined face. "What are you waiting on?"

"I was wondering what this says—"

He threw his hands up and sat back. "With what I'm paying you, I figured you could read just fine."

Her irritation mounted, but she shoved it down. "Well, Dr. Edwards, I still haven't figured out your notations. So, if you'd take a look, I can take care of Frisky."

He nodded. "Miss Francis's tabby?"

"Yes," she ground out. "She's here for an exam."

He tapped the note. "Reminder for me to pick up fresh green beans on the way home for Mrs. Edwards." He chuckled. "Don't think I remembered."

Tandy had carried the file back into the exam room.

She'd done her best to stay professional with Miss Francis, but she was close to tears—of frustration. No wonder Dr. Edwards was paying so well. She was pretty sure it wasn't worth it.

Since the office needed a good cleaning, she'd come in on her first Saturday wearing rubber gloves and toting bleach water. Everything felt dirty and gritty. Lucky for her, Renata and Scarlett had offered to help. Of course, once they'd stepped inside, they'd almost bailed on her.

"Looks better," Scarlett said now, leaning on her mop.

"When I planned to take some vacation time, I hadn't intended to do so much work. First helping out at Fire Gorge. Now this. Man, next time I'm taking a cruise or something." Renata sighed. "I'm beginning to miss Stonewall Crossing and my job."

"Ooh, a cruise sounds like fun," Scarlett said.

"Doesn't it?" Renata grinned. "Just the three of us. I bet I can take off some more time after the next high season. How soon do you think you can take some time off?" Renata loved her job at the Stonewall Crossing Tourism Department—doing whatever it took to help put her hometown on the map as a top Texas tourist stop.

Tandy laughed. "A while. I don't know what I'd do without you two," she said, pushing the cabinet drawer. It hung on the rails twice, making her shove a little harder. It slammed shut, knocking the pile of manila folders stacked precariously on top to the floor. She stared at the mess, overwhelmed and deflated. She stooped, piling the manila folders back up and slapping them on the file cabinet.

"It's not too late to leave," Renata said. "I'm heading home tomorrow. I can make room."

"I gave up my job at the vet hospital," she argued,

feeling like a fool. Why had she agreed to this? "My replacement is terrific—I trained him myself."

"Still…" Scarlett glanced at the filing cabinet. "After the veterinary hospital, this is like…"

"Stepping back in time?" Renata finished. "Yeah, this is bad."

Tandy didn't disagree. But what did she have to go back to? Babysitting her nieces and nephews. Being the third wheel with her brother and his family? Being the single one. Well, she and Renata were both single. But Tandy knew it was because her cousin hadn't found the right man yet. Renata wasn't broken inside like she was. Renata would find love, and it would be deep and real and forever.

"Hate to break up this party, but we're working tonight," Scarlett said to Renata.

Tandy looked around the cramped office. "I think we've done all we can do."

"Does that mean we're finally leaving?" Renata smiled. "Because I think you owe us ice cream."

Banshee perked up from his place on the floor.

"See, even Banshee agrees," Renata added.

Tandy laughed. "I could go for ice cream. And some fresh air. Come on, Banshee, let's get these ladies their payment." She led them from the clinic, locking up behind them and testing the door before they walked down the corner and took a right. "Come by my place after you're done? I'll have lots of ice cream."

"How's the cabin?" Scarlett asked.

"I haven't spent much time there," she said. "I get here, work late, go home and collapse in bed."

"Because your new boss is a slave driver or because you're avoiding your neighbor?" Renata asked, grinning.

Tandy frowned. "I'm not avoiding anyone. How can you avoid someone in a town this small?"

"Kind of like you avoiding the question?" Renata asked.

She shook her head, trying not to react. "What is there to avoid?"

Renata and Scarlett exchanged a long look.

"That he loves you?" Scarlett asked.

"That there's something going on, I'm thinking seriously wrong, with his current situation?" Renata added.

Tandy blew out a deep breath, hating how well they knew one another. She'd been thinking the same thing. Not about him caring about her—that hadn't crossed her mind. But the rest of it, yes. "I'm supposed to fix it? The situation, not your delusion that he still cares about me."

They exchanged another look.

"Stop it." But Tandy couldn't hold back the laugh. She was so tired, it felt good to laugh. Laughing was a superior reaction to crying. "You two could talk to him, you know. You're his friends just as much as I am."

Renata rolled her eyes. "Please, Tandy." She shook her head. "Your name is tattooed on his body. Yours. Not mine. Not Scarlett. I'm thinking, since you have prime real estate on that holy-wow body, you're special."

Holy wow was right. She'd tried to hang curtains over the view of Lynnie's house, but the wall had wood rot and the curtain rod collapsed to the floor. She'd seen him each night, walking the porch and in her dreams. Some nights she'd had to take a cold shower to ease the ache he caused.

"Whatever," she said. "See you later."

"You better get a lot of ice cream," Renata called out, climbing into Scarlett's small SUV.

She waved and pushed into the Old Town Soda

Shoppe, eager to move on to another topic. Instead, she saw Click sitting at a table, Pearl in a high chair across from him.

"Ta-dee!" Pearl yelled. "Da-gee!" She clapped.

Tandy waved back.

Click had been bent over the table, propped on his elbow. Pearl's declaration had him jerking upright.

Was he sleeping? She crossed the store, truly concerned by Click's appearance. His eyes were bloodshot, a heavy stubble covered his jaw and his normally starched-and-pressed appearance...wasn't.

"When did you sleep last?" she asked, giving him a thorough once-over. He looked worn out and then some. "You okay?"

He ran a hand over his face. "I'm good."

She stared at him. She'd done her best not to think about him this week. He hadn't texted for that walk, and she wasn't going to make the offer twice. But seeing him this way stirred a twinge of guilt.

"You don't look *good.*" *Don't get involved. Don't ask questions. Smile and leave.* She wasn't responsible for him or Pearl... But she was sitting down, smiling at Banshee as he sat next to Pearl's high chair. He endured her sticky-finger pats, his long tongue lapping up any ice cream lingering on Pearl's little hands. "How are you, Pearl? Having ice cream?" she asked.

"She's a mess," Click said, as if only now seeing his daughter. She *was* a mess, sticky and sweet and adorable. Nothing to get worked up over. But he was pushing out of his chair.

"Sit down before you fall down, Click," Tandy said gently, giving up the fight. For Pearl. She drew in a deep breath. "Let me help. I've probably earned a million-plus fieldwork hours with my cousins' kids."

"A million plus?" He sat, his jaw locking as he glanced her way. "You're working just as many hours as I am."

Meaning he'd been keeping tabs on her, too?

"It's a new job," she said, her only explanation. He didn't need to hear about it, that much was clear. "You can't take care of Pearl if you're not taking care of yourself." She dug through the diaper bag, finding the wipes and pulling two out. She grinned at Pearl as she wiped the remaining stickiness from her pink cheeks and the tip of her little nose. Banshee had already taken care of the ice cream, but Tandy wiped down her fingers and hands all the same. "Thanks for the help, Banshee."

Click ran another hand over his face, stifling a yawn.

"Click?" she asked. "What's going on?"

His shoulders drooped, his gaze fixed on the glass of melted ice cream. From the whipped cream and cherry floating on top, it had once been a sundae of some sort. "I've had Pearl for…" He paused, staring at the ceiling. "…thirteen days? Two weeks? It's all starting to run together."

"You normally just have her for weekends?" she asked. "Guess that's the normal custody arrangement."

Click shook his head. "No. I mean, I wouldn't know."

Her chest grew tight and heavy. "Did Pearl's mom… Did she die?" she whispered, looking at the baby. Click had seen more than his fair share of loss.

He shook his head.

She was relieved, yet confused. Until the pieces fell into place. "You mean this is the only time you've had her—*ever*?" Tandy asked. It was the only thing that made sense. Click didn't have that natural comfort level a father develops with time. Not for a baby this age. He was scared, uncertain, but doing the best he could. But why?

He wasn't the sort to turn his back on his obligations. Well, not the Click she'd thought she'd known.

His gaze fixed on his daughter. He cleared his throat. "Pearl's mom is in rehab. She told me I was a father right before she left Pearl with me."

He hadn't known? And now, he was on his own? Caregiver to a baby he barely knew...

Tandy couldn't breathe, couldn't think. The thudding of her heart drowned out all other sounds. Why had the woman kept it a secret? Poor Pearl. She'd been robbed of so much time with her father. And Click. She glanced at him. He was so lost.

"You've got no help?" she asked, the answer on his face.

"I was coming to Lynnie. I figured she'd set me straight, show me what needs doing for Pearl. But now..." He shook his head.

Now Lynnie was gone. She swallowed, stunned by the burn of tears.

"There's a lot to be done. When Pearl sleeps, I do what needs to be done. Repairs to the barn and fence. The horses... Horses need tending to. I can't leave her alone." He grinned at Pearl. "She's busy, into everything."

Tandy sat back in her chair, processing. Questions circled, so many questions. And yes, most of them weren't relevant at the moment. Neither was how she did or didn't feel about Click. Or how he did or didn't feel about her. What mattered was this little girl. "Scarlett and I can help, Click." She didn't have to ask, she knew Scarlett would be on board.

"It's not your problem," he argued. "I'm not looking for a handout." Click straightened in his chair, but it took effort.

She frowned. "It's no handout. She'll be the one that

suffers when you collapse from exhaustion. This is for her." She tickled Pearl's cheek. "I can think of worse things than spending time with her."

Pearl clapped her hands.

"Exactly," she said. "Pearl approves."

Click grinned, then yawned.

"You need sleep." She'd never seen him so worn out.

He shook his head. "Gotta finish the patch of fence first. Damn goats are escape artists. Almost done."

"It'd take a third of the time if you'd get some help," she offered. "I could ask around, see if any of Uncle Woodrow's ranch hands are looking for extra hours?"

"No offense, but I'm pretty sure your uncle wouldn't want any of his people working for me." One dark brow arched. "He hasn't figured out what to do with me yet."

Tandy agreed. "Not everyone works for my uncle. Or Mr. Wallace." She paused then, curious. "What do you mean, what to do with you?"

"How to get Lynnie's place. Since she left it to me. All of it," he said. "Both Wallace and Boone have wanted the place so long, I'm worried it could get nasty."

She smiled. Lynnie had done the right thing. He wouldn't have expected her generosity, but he'd appreciate it in a way that few could. "What are they going to do? It's the twenty-first century. No one's poisoning water holes or rustling cattle anymore, are they?"

The smile he sent her way was devastating. How could a man look so vulnerable and so proud all at the same time? And the look in his eyes... His gaze traveled over her face, shifting into something else. He was wide awake now, his gaze falling to her mouth. She knew that look, knew what he was thinking and wanting. Her. It rippled over her, causing a full-body shudder.

"Ta-dee," Pearl squealed, reaching for her. "Hi."

"Hi, pretty Pearl," she said, pulling her from her high chair. The toddler twined her arms around Tandy's neck and rested her head on her shoulder.

"Ta-dee," she said with a sigh.

Tandy held Pearl close, soaking up every ounce of affection. She stared at Click over Pearl's head. "Lynnie's given you a gift, Click. You can stay now, have a real home."

She wasn't prepared for the intensity in those blue-green eyes. Or the way her stomach tightened in response to his husky, "Maybe."

"Maybe?" she repeated, confused. Surely he wasn't having second thoughts because of her? She might not be a part of it anymore, but she wouldn't take his dream away from him. She wouldn't do that to Pearl.

"Da da." Pearl reached for him.

He reached for Pearl, the brush of his hands against hers making her ache. She'd always felt cherished in his arms. He'd managed to chase away her doubt and uncertainty, made things steady and right. What she wouldn't give to feel that way now. In that moment, she wished he still loved her. That she could trust in their love and know he'd always be with her. That she was strong enough to let go and brave enough to try again.

"Ta-dee. Da-gee. Yum-yum." Pearl was chattering, pointing at things as she went. "Da da."

"That's me," Click said, kissing her little fingertip.

This little girl had every right to a good life, full of love and stability. Lynnie might not have known about Pearl, but she'd wanted Click's future to be secure. "You owe it to your daughter, Click. Give her a legacy she'll be proud of."

CLICK TRIED TO argue when Tandy followed him back to Lynnie's place. He tried to argue when she told him to take a shower and go to bed. He tried to argue when she rummaged through the refrigerator, looking for something to make for dinner. But when she put Pearl on her lap and opened Lynnie's piano, he didn't say a word.

The wonder on Pearl's face was awe inspiring. He leaned against the door frame, watching her tiny fingers hover over the ivory keys. Tandy played one song, then another. Pearl sat, her hands folded in her lap, watching closely. When the song ended, Pearl clapped and clapped. So did he.

"You're supposed to be taking a shower. And a nap," Tandy said. "Tell Daddy to go to night-night, Pearl. Say night-night, Daddy."

Pearl shook her head, giggling.

"No?" Tandy said. "You want Daddy to make music?"

"Mew-sik!" Pearl said. "Da da."

He laughed. "Tandy's the musician, Pearl. I might be able to hammer out chopsticks."

Tandy slid over.

"Da da," Pearl whispered, clapping her hands again.

He sat, his weariness melting away when both Pearl and Tandy stared at him. "Here goes." He held his hands over the keys, waved them in the air and shook his head.

Pearl patted his arm.

He nodded and started playing. He fumbled through it, turning it into a show for Pearl more than a serious attempt to produce music. Pearl was too delighted to care. And Tandy... She was laughing along with Pearl. "You're up," he said to Tandy, glad to be done.

Tandy played a song he'd never heard before, the notes soft and light and carefree. When she started singing, he and Pearl stared at her.

"Time for bed, little one, time to dream

Close your eyes, cuddle close, and sleep sweet

Rest your head, little one, rest easy
Sail away on white clouds, and dream deep."

Tandy kept playing, her fingers coaxing the sooth-ing melody from the piano keys. Click watched her fin-gers, her hands, the way her body swayed slightly to the music. And Pearl, Pearl looked at Tandy like she was an angel. Her bright eyes stayed on Tandy's face, her little rosebud mouth mimicking Tandy silently. When Tandy played the song again, Pearl put her hand on Tandy's arm.

Tandy's smile wavered ever so slightly, reminding him of how hard this must be for her. He ached to com-fort her, to hold her while she cried. She'd had no one to hold her while she grieved for their baby. He'd let her chase him away, leaving her alone with her mother—and he hated himself for it. Susan Boone had no heart. And he'd left Tandy in her care. If Tandy held on to her grief and guarded her heart, it was his fault as much as her mother's.

Pearl relaxed against him, her little hand sliding from Tandy's arm as she drifted off into sleep. Tandy nod-ded, shooting him a sweet smile when their eyes met. He turned Pearl into his shoulder and stood, carrying her across the parlor and down the hall to their bedroom.

He placed Pearl in her bed and stared down at her. Poor Pearl. One minute she'd had a mother, of sorts. The next, she had him. Did Pearl miss her? From what Geor-gia's roommate had told him, she'd been a good mother—as good as expected for a drug addict. He could do this on his own. He had to. Hell, seeing the damage Tandy's mother had done, he knew having a bad parent could be worse than having none. Would Georgia come back for her? Did he want her to?

He straightened, rubbing the names inked on his arm. It was pointless to wish for the impossible. That family—

him and Tandy and Pearl—could never be. And yet, for one brief moment, he let the warmth of that idea wash over him. There would be so much love there.

He smoothed the blanket over Pearl and walked down the hall, listening to Tandy play. He took his time, wanting to delay the inevitable change that Pearl's absence would bring. There was a gulf between them, so deep and wide, he didn't see a way around it. Still, he was willing to try.

She broke off when he entered the room, pushing off the piano bench and looking at him. "How long will she sleep?"

He shrugged. "An hour. Maybe two."

"So you can nap?" she asked, crossing her arms over her chest—warning him away.

With no Pearl between them, all the things said and unsaid crowded in on him. But, maybe, things didn't have to stay unsaid. He cleared his throat. Where the hell to start?

"I came here to help you with Pearl," she said, as if sensing his thoughts. "You should sleep."

He shook his head. "Not yet." He drew in a deep breath, searching her face. "How's the job?"

She relaxed a little, her gaze wandering out the front window. "I think I might have bitten off more than I can chew."

He chuckled. "Doubt that."

She arched a brow. "I don't. I don't know how the place has been functioning." Her gaze locked with this. "But I'll figure things out. And now you're going to take a nap."

"Haven't had much adult conversation in the last week," he said.

She nodded, a small smile on her mouth. "She's smart.

Soon enough, you'll miss her gibberish. Once she starts talking, there's no going back." Her smile faded slowly.

"Nice to have company," he said, watching her face. He'd missed her, so damn much.

She tore her gaze from his, tucking a strand of long blond hair behind her ear. "Toben's a father, too. A son." She paused, closing the lid on the piano. Her fingers stroked the wood with such affection, he was almost jealous. "Rowdy."

"Great name," he said. "Sounds about right, too, if he's anything like Toben."

Her smile was back. She loved her brother. But once their gazes met, that guarded awareness was there. Blazing. And Click couldn't take it anymore. "Tandy, there're things to be said—"

"No." Her voice razor sharp, she threw up a hand.

"Tandy—"

"We're not talking about the past." The words were harsh.

He gritted his teeth. "Let me apologize."

She shook her head, her eyes narrowing. "It doesn't matter."

"It does, dammit," he argued.

"You need to apologize so I need to listen?" She shook her head. "So *you* can feel better? Be able to let go and move on?"

He tore his gaze from hers, staring at the floor. If he thought she was happy, that she'd moved on, he'd let it go. But she hadn't. And neither had he. Maybe together they could find a way back to living without bearing so much pain. He sucked in a deep breath and stared at her. "Have you?" He crossed the room, needing to be close to her. Yearning for her touch. "I can't. I don't want to."

Her eyes went round. "Click…" She seemed to wilt, her skin paling.

"I'm sorry I left you." He gripped her shoulders. "I was out of my head, losing Amelia. Losing you." He pulled her close. "I didn't know what to do or say to keep you."

Tears filled her eyes but she blinked them back. "Click." His name, from her lips, gutted him.

"It wasn't your fault," he whispered. "You know that."

She was shaking her head, her eyes pressed shut.

"It wasn't, Tandy," he pleaded, his hold tightening. "Dammit. There was nothing you could have done." No matter what the doctor had told them, the damage had been done. Susan Boone's question had echoed in that hospital room, "What did she do to make this happen?" He'd stared at the woman, speechless. But the question planted a seed, one that took hold of Tandy's grief and twisted it into something hard and crippling. His father had been a bastard, but Tandy's mother was a real-life flesh-and-blood monster. "No matter what your mom said, you have to know. I never thought it was your fault, never blamed you. You hear me? But I blame myself for leaving."

She tried to pull away, her eyes still closed tightly.

The pain on her face almost shut him up. But if he didn't say it, she'd never know. "I'm sorry I didn't stay until you believed that, too."

She was shaking.

"I hold on to that time because what we shared was real." He smoothed her hair from her shoulder, savoring the slip of silk against his fingertips. "She was real and perfect—"

She covered her ears, shaking her head frantically. "Stop. Please stop." She shrugged away from him. "What do you want? You need me to tell you I believe you? Fine,

I do. You want me to tell you I'm not mad at you?" She waited, desperation lining her face. "I'm not mad. I told you to go, to move on. You did." She choked on the last word, more potent that a slap to the face.

He stared at her, her anguish hard to watch.

"What words do I need to say to make you stop talking about her? I can't." She shook her head and stepped away from him. She pressed a hand to her chest. *"I can't."* She slammed out the front door.

He'd pushed too hard, too fast. Instead of making things better he'd made them worse. But her wild desperation tore his heart out. Had she ever grieved their baby girl? Made peace with her passing? Or had her guilt stolen that from her, too? He should have kept his damn mouth shut and held her close. He should have told her he loved her. And that he always would.

Chapter Ten

"Should hit soon," Dr. Edwards said, peering out the front window for the eleventh time that morning.

She nodded, ignoring the old man.

The last couple of weeks had seen a smattering of electrical storms and howling winds. While she'd been wearing herself out doing her *and* Doc Edwards's work, helping out with Pearl while avoiding Click, and lending the occasional hand—and guitar—at Fire Gorge, Dr. Edwards spent hours staring out the window proclaiming the imminent arrival of a funnel cloud. But, thankfully, not one tornado.

"It's not tornado season," she murmured, opening the file drawer.

Dr. Edwards chuckled. "It's always tornado season hereabouts, missy," he said. "You listen to an old man and get your fanny home, and soon."

She looked at him. "We have patients waiting." She glanced at the clock. It was barely two in the afternoon.

"Those damn sirens always go off too late," he said, as if she hadn't spoken. "John Mason's whole barn was sucked clean up into a twister before the damn sirens went off."

She glanced out the window. "When was that?"

"Oh, let's see, back in eighty-eight, I guess." He shrugged.

The sky was red with dust, the wind rattling the glass in their panes. But that didn't mean much. "What makes you think we'll see a tornado today?" It was the same question she'd asked at least five times in the last two weeks. He always had a different reason, each one more interesting than the last.

"My left knee," he said.

She frowned. That was disappointing. "Well, let me know when it's about time and I'll—"

"Doc Edwards," Charlene called out. "Tommy Juarez just called, from over in Alpine. Said they've had two touch down in the last couple of minutes."

He nodded. "You know the drill."

Tandy didn't. "What's the drill?"

"Charlene sends them all home," he said. "Tommy wouldn't have called if they weren't coming this a'way. You get yourself on home, you here? We got this."

She sighed, closed the drawer and looked at Banshee. He stood, staring out the window. That got her attention. She made sure all the kennels were secure before grabbing her keys. "See you tomorrow," she said on her way out the door.

The town looked closed up tight as she and Banshee climbed into her truck and headed to her cabin. They were pushed this way and that on the road, the gusts shaking her nerves more than once. Still, she didn't want to get caught out on a flat road with nothing to hide behind. It was only as they were pulling into their drive that she realized they had no storm cellar.

She pushed the door open and braced it with her leg, letting Banshee slip out first. She followed, reaching back for her bag. The wind slammed into the door, pushing it into the back of her head and shoulder, making her see stars.

"Shit," she called out, leaning against the cab and pressing a hand to the back of her head. Banshee whimpered, circling her. "It's okay," she said, holding on to the truck bed to stay upright.

The wind roared like an out-of-control freight train.

Banshee started barking. He whined, then ran off, barking furiously.

"Banshee?" She blinked, staring into the thick red air. No sign of him. She couldn't see much through the dust clouds. If he'd left her in search of shelter, she didn't blame him. She clung to the truck bed, reaching back to probe the lump on the back of her head. "You're fine," she murmured. There was blood. She shook her head, but that hurt, too.

The wind carried sound to her, distorted and wavering. She heard Banshee, but he sounded far away. Someone was yelling? And that damn roaring wind. She needed to get inside. Banshee needed to get inside. The damn cabin had lasted this long, she'd hope it would make it through this time.

"Banshee!" she called, but the wind whipped it away. She clung to the truck, a sudden gust of wind kicking up dust and making it near impossible to see. Up until now, she'd dismissed Dr. Edwards's announcement. But now, now she was beginning to panic.

"Banshee?" she yelled, letting go of the truck and staggering a few steps. She was light-headed. Probably a concussion. Great. She just needed to make it to the house.

The wind died suddenly, an eerie quiet falling.

"Tandy?" Click called out, running through the tall grass to get to her.

"Click?" She wavered, too dizzy to react or move

quickly. "I hit my head," she called out when he was closer. "Concussion, I think."

He was there, in front of her, staring down at her. "I'm carrying you," he said, scooping her up before she could protest. Not that she was going to protest. The world seemed too off-kilter to move. And now was one of those times when they needed to move.

But Click had bigger responsibilities. "Pearl?" she stiffened, panicking.

"Scarlett has her in the storm cellar," he said, holding her close against his chest as he hurried back across the grass. "Where we're going."

Her relief was instantaneous. So was her temper. "Why the hell are you out here? You have a daughter to think of."

"You're welcome," he said.

By the time they reached the storm cellar, the wind had picked up again. It was worse this time, the dirt and grit stinging her cheeks and blinding them. She hung on to Click, knowing she was safe in his arms. He was stumbling forward, somehow managing to stay on his feet. Were they moving? She couldn't tell.

"About time," Scarlett said as they descended the concrete steps into the storm cellar.

Tandy wiped her eyes, coughing and sneezing and grabbing the back of her head. The deafening roar of the wind stopped, signaling Click had closed the doors.

Banshee's nose pressed against her chest, his deep-chested rumble making it easier to breathe.

"Good to see you, too," she said, stroking his broad neck.

"He came to get Click," Scarlett said. "Good thing, too, we were about to shut the doors."

"Ta-dee?" Pearl asked, her little hands gripping hers before Tandy could truly see.

"Hi, Pearl," she managed, wiping her eyes until it was easier to focus. "Hi, sweet cuddle bunny." She blinked, still coughing, until she could see. It was surprisingly bright in the small concrete room.

Click kneeled in front of her on the ground. "You doing okay?" he asked, his gaze searching hers.

"Fine," she said, wishing she meant it. Her head was throbbing and, if the wet sensation on the back of her neck wasn't sweat, still bleeding.

"Don't lie to me, Tandy." His tone was harsh.

She blinked, startled by the severity of the concern in his voice. "Any water?" she whispered.

A water bottle was pressed into her hand.

"Bandana?" she asked. "Towel?"

"Sorry," Scarlett said, shaking her head.

She nodded. Now that things were a little clearer, she knew her head was bleeding. And throbbing. "I think I need stitches. My head." She winced as her fingers probed through her hair. When she held her hand out, her fingers were covered in blood.

"Oh, Tandy." Scarlett's eyes went round.

"I'm wearing a T-shirt underneath. It's probably still clean enough to hold against the cut." She unbuttoned a button of her blouse, but the pain in her shoulder made it difficult. "I hurt my shoulder, too. I need some help."

"Ta-dee?" Pearl said.

Banshee whimpered.

"I'm okay." She smiled at the baby girl. "Are we playing hide-and-seek from the wind?"

Click unbuttoned his shirt and tugged it off. "Hold this, Pearl?" he asked, smiling as Pearl wrapped it around her like a robe.

Pearl giggled, spinning around.

"Looks good," he said, shrugging out of his undershirt. "Fresh out of the dryer." He offered her the white cotton undershirt. "Pearl and I did laundry this morning."

But Tandy was having a hell of a hard time concentrating again. Only this time it had nothing to do with the pain in her head. Instead it was all Click and the wall of muscle that was his amazing chest—within her reach. He was far too tempting a specimen. Being this close, wrapped in his scent, made it impossible to think.

Or it was the concussion?

Her gaze wandered, exploring every familiar inch.

His tattoo, the only mark on his beautiful body, circled the muscles of his upper arm. Her name. On his skin. She no longer had a right to him, yet the ownership was there—warming her through. The urge to trace her name burned her fingertips. But it vanished when she looked closer. There were more lines now, smaller, detailed. Spelling out…

Amelia.

Her lungs seemed to collapse in on themselves. The pain in her head paled as the agony in her chest blossomed, encompassing every inch of her until she couldn't contain it. Her gaze met his as she collapsed against him, pressing his shirt to her mouth to muffle her sobs.

HE COULDN'T BREATHE. His chest was wet with her tears, her shoulders shaking as she sobbed. He stared at the concrete bunker wall, trying to think of the right thing to do. With Pearl, Banshee and Scarlett watching. Holding her seemed right.

"Ta-dee?" Pearl's voice was soft.

"I've got Tandy, Pearl," he said, smiling down at his daughter.

Pearl smiled, patting his hip. "Da da." She toddled back to Scarlett.

"That's right, Daddy's taking care of Tandy," Scarlett said, gathering his daughter into her lap. "Let's read a book. A doggie book?"

Pearl nodded.

Thankfulness washed over him. For Pearl and Tandy, Scarlett and Lynnie—even Banshee. Times like this made him realize how much he had to be thankful for. Tandy had been as good as her word. She and Scarlett had alternated shifts, showing up whenever they could. Making dinner, bathing Pearl or cleaning up so he could get some work done on the property. Scarlett always talked his ear off, but Tandy was only interested in conversing with Pearl. He gave her space, coming inside long enough to hear Tandy sing his daughter to sleep. Something about her lullabies eased the ache inside him. For a while. Bottom line, if he'd been alone with Pearl today, if Scarlett hadn't been on hand to take care of his daughter, Tandy would be outside right now.

His heart thundered in his chest, overcome by what could have happened...

But hadn't. She was here, in his arms, a little battered but here. His hands slid up her back to cradle her close. She shivered and burrowed closer, her breath fanning across his chest. If she hadn't been bleeding, he'd have stayed this way. As it was, she needed tending to.

"Tandy," he murmured. "Your head."

She pressed the shirt against his hand, then slid her arms around his waist.

"That works," he whispered in her ear. He smoothed her hair aside, wincing at the gash in the back of her head. She'd need stitches all right, but there wasn't a damn thing he could do about that now. He placed his shirt over her wound and pressed.

She pressed her face into his chest, but he heard her soft cry.

"I'm sorry," he whispered, not wanting to hurt her. He was no doctor, but applying pressure to the wound was the only hope they had to slow or stop the bleeding for now. Still, he tried to be careful.

"It's okay," she murmured back. "Thank you."

She didn't need to thank him. Everything he'd done, he'd done for himself. She was essential to him. The world outside shook, flattening homes and threatening livelihoods. But Click wasn't worried. He'd found his purpose. It was right here, with Pearl and Tandy. They were safe and protected, so he was happy. Life was truly that simple.

Tandy sniffed, her breath escaping on a long shudder. The gash on her head probably hurt like hell. He ran his hand up and down her back, offering her the only comfort he had. Her fingers pressed into his back, gripping him tightly, holding him in place. Not like he was going anywhere.

He'd known a tornado was coming since this morning. There was a stillness outside, as if all the air had been sucked up for use later. Scarlett had shown up after breakfast, giving Click the chance to check the storm cellar. As always, Lynnie was prepared. Tornado or no, he had no reason to worry.

Until he saw Banshee. The dog had barked and barked, grabbing his shirt and tugging him toward the fence line. He'd closed Scarlett and Pearl inside the storm cellar with Banshee, then run. Tandy was in trouble.

His arms tightened around her now, assuring him she was safe. He sucked in a deep breath and shifted, sitting on the bench and cradling her against his chest. He kept the shirt tucked tight behind her head, making sure her injury was covered. This way he could see her. And, dammit, he wanted to see her.

Those hazel-green eyes of hers stared up at him. "You shouldn't have come after me," she whispered.

"No?" he asked, cocking an eyebrow.

"No."

He grinned. She knew, she had to know. "No choice, Tandy. When it comes to you, I've never had one."

Those eyes fluttered, surprised. As if his revelation was new information. How could she have doubted that? No matter what had happened, what might happen, he'd love her till the day he died. And he was fine with it. Hell, more than fine with it. Being with her was the only time things felt *right*.

"Ta-dee?" Pearl asked, climbing down from Scarlett's lap.

Tandy turned, wincing at the slight motion.

"Stop moving, woman." Click sighed. "She's okay, Pearl."

"Some kisses might help," Scarlett said. "Give her kisses, Pearl?"

Pearl smiled, standing on tiptoe to plant a kiss on Tandy's cheek.

"Thank you, Pearl. I feel better already," Tandy said, but she didn't move.

"Da da." Pearl pointed at Tandy. "Ki."

"Ki? Kiss?" He swallowed.

Pearl nodded.

He cleared his throat. "You want me to kiss Tandy?"

Pearl nodded, waiting expectantly. How could he refuse?

"You see what you started?" Tandy said to Scarlett, making him chuckle.

"Da da," Pearl repeated.

He heard Tandy's breath waver as he bent close. No way to rush these things. His nose trailed along her temple, drawing her scent in. He loved the way she smelled, loved the warm softness of her skin, and the taste of her lips. Nothing compared to Tandy in his arms. He dreamed about it still. He pressed a kiss to her forehead, keeping in mind their very watchful audience.

Pearl clapped, her giggle inspiring Banshee to cover his tiny daughter's face with slobbery kisses.

"Good boy," he said, meaning it. Damn dog was a hero in his book. If he hadn't barked, Tandy would have been stuck out there. His arms tightened, holding her closer to ease the sharp twisting of his heart.

Scarlett cleared her throat. "I'm feeling like a third wheel here," she said.

He frowned. "There're five of us in here."

She shook her head. "Fine, be obtuse. I just don't get you two. So... How's work, Tandy?"

Tandy sighed, her eyes shut. "Okay."

"You're not supposed to sleep," he said, a hint of warning in his voice.

Her eyes popped open. "Who's sleeping?" she asked, the look in her eyes taking him by surprise.

He wasn't the only one grappling with the effect they had on each other. The flare of hunger in her gaze sent a jolt straight to his spine. Every nerve jumped and hummed to life.

"You decide what you're going to do yet, Click?" Scarlett asked.

News of his inheritance had only just gone public. In that time, neither Wallace nor Boone had reached out to him. Probably waiting to see who made the first move. "Still working on it. But good call, sending me to the tourism department. Best way to find the local businesses if you're an outsider like me. Mr. Delgado's men know their stuff. Had the fences fixed in no time. And the barn is almost ready for horses—if any were to come visit." It was what he wanted, deep down he knew it was. Having a home and the business he'd always dreamed of? For Click, it was too good to be true.

"And will there be visitors?" Tandy asked. Was it his imagination or did she sound excited? "A training facility for cutting horses, here? Lynnie's place is big enough, isn't it?"

He nodded. It was—and then some. "Do I want to raise Pearl here? Surrounded by folks that might never accept her?"

Tandy frowned up at him. "So they win? What about you?"

"I won't make out so bad if I sell." He chuckled. Still the idea sat wrong. How could he sell? How could he lose the only tie he had to the woman he'd loved and admired. "I keep waiting. Things like this don't happen for people like me." He hadn't meant to say that last bit out loud.

"People like you?" Tandy asked. "Hardworking? Responsible?"

"Loyal and kind," Scarlett added. "I wish you could see you the way we do, Click. I know your upbringing was rough. But you aren't."

Tandy pressed a hand to his chest. "Listen to her," she murmured. Her gaze was fixed on her hand. Was it the out-of-control pounding of his heart that held her fascination? Or something else?

"I think you should stay," Scarlett spoke up. "Is...is Pearl's mom not coming back?" She glanced at Pearl, sitting on the floor beside Banshee and flipping through her board books.

"I don't know," he answered honestly.

"You have someplace to go? Work that's waiting on you?" Scarlett asked. "If not, think on it a while. You'll figure out what's best for you and Pearl."

He nodded, his attention wandering back to the woman in his arms. Tandy looked pale, too pale. He nodded at Scarlett. "Check the radio. See if it's safe to get Tandy to a hospital."

Scarlett hopped up, turning on the old weather radio. It was some time before they announced the all clear. Once they did, he helped Tandy sit on the bench and peeked through the storm cellar doors. Nothing out of the ordinary. He cracked the door then pushed it wide, climbing up and out of the cellar to take stock of the damage.

The grass was flattened, an odd swirling pattern cutting across part of his property. The fence between him and Tandy's cabin was curled back into a tangled knot of cedar posts and barbed wire. Beyond that was what remained of Tandy's cabin.

His heart sank. Her truck had smashed through the back, bringing the structure down on top of it.

If Banshee hadn't come to him, she'd be dead. The blood seemed to drain from him, leaving him numb. As far as Click was concerned, Banshee had earned a T-bone steak for the rest of the week. Hell, the month.

Lynnie's home—his home—was still standing. One window was broken, but there were no other visible signs of damage. The barn, too.

"You were lucky," Scarlett said, peering out. "I should check in with the family, so they know I'm okay. I can keep Pearl," she added. "That way you can take Tandy in to get her head patched up."

Ten minutes later, Pearl and Scarlett were headed to Fire Gorge and he was driving Tandy and Banshee into town. As they drove the debris-covered road into Fort Kyle, he gazed out the windows, looking for damage or anyone needing help. Considering how vast the Wallace and Boone properties were, there weren't many homesteads to worry over.

He kept asking Tandy questions, hoping to keep her focused. In the big picture, a concussion wasn't a big deal. He'd had a couple in his lifetime. But the headaches were no fun. And, if he remembered it correctly, there was a general fog of disorientation and dizziness.

He glanced at her, wanting to take her hand and comfort her—and himself.

She looked his way, her big eyes studying his face. Her smile was unexpected, and beautiful. He smiled back, shaking his head.

"What?" she asked.

"Been a long time since you smiled at me like that." He swallowed back the lump in his throat.

"Must be the concussion," she said, giggling.

He chuckled, too, turning onto Main Street and navigating the short distance to the hospital. It was surprisingly quiet. But then, the locals knew how to handle a tornado. He signed Tandy in and followed her gurney back. No way he was going to sit in that damn waiting room. He'd left her once when she needed him. He wasn't about to do it again.

Chapter Eleven

Tandy was tired of resting. For two days, Scarlett had hovered. If Scarlett wasn't, then Renata was calling her on the phone. Aunt Evelyn was relentless… Tandy had pretended to sleep twice just to avoid her. She meant well, but Tandy couldn't shake the feeling she was being interrogated. About who and what, she wasn't sure. But her aunt was looking for something. Hell, even Tobyn had called and texted. She appreciated their concern, but she truly was fine.

Other than her cabin and truck, a storage facility and a car lot a county over, the tornado hadn't left too much damage. While everyone was getting back to normal activities, she was trapped in Scarlett's bed. Banshee was just as stir-crazy as she was, tugging her blankets and scratching the door. "Agreed," she said to the dog. The doctor had said twenty-four to forty-eight hours of rest. She was calling it.

As soon as Scarlett left for the afternoon kid activities, Tandy kicked back the covers and got dressed. Banshee's tail was wagging a mile a minute when she pulled open the door. And came face-to-face with Click and Pearl.

The last time she'd seen Click he'd been dusty and worn out, all but chased from the hospital by her aunt and uncle. Uncle Woodrow had wasted no time pointing out that he wasn't family. She'd tried to argue, but Click had said, "Doc said quiet is what you need. I'll check on you later." He'd shot her a wink and slipped out.

She'd missed him. And Pearl. She'd stared at her phone a time or two but couldn't bring herself to text him.

Now he was all pressed and starched, freshly shaven and smelling downright delicious. She swallowed, bombarded by a million conflicting emotions and sensations she wasn't quite ready to face.

"Ta-dee!" Pearl said, grinning from ear to ear. "Butter?"

"Hi, precious Pearl." She stooped, hugging the toddler close. "How are you?"

Pearl nodded. "Ta-dee butter?"

"She looks better," Click said. "How do you feel?"

"Oh, better?" Tandy stood. "Yes, feeling much better. Thank you, Pearl."

Click held out a huge bouquet of wildflowers. "Pearl picked them for you."

"Ba-shee," Pearl said, hugging the dog.

"Listen to you." Tandy shook her head, taking the bouquet. "Banshee's happy to see you, too. Thank you for the pretty flowers."

"Making a break for it?" Click asked.

She frowned, suspicion creeping in. "Did Scarlett tell you to come babysit?"

He shook his head. "Nope. We wanted to see you. And Banshee." He nodded at Pearl, still hugging Banshee.

Tandy smiled. "I need some fresh air. And space." She pointed at the small suite Scarlett called home. "I don't know where I'm going. Just out."

"We can help you with that." His grin went straight to her heart.

The last two days had been filled with thoughts of

him. His blue-green eyes, the strength in his arms and his tattoo. She'd felt so locked in grief, convinced she was at fault for losing Amelia...convinced he'd never be able to look at her without resentment. Shutting him out had made it easier to shut out the truth: she'd lost everything—including hope.

It might be easier to keep everyone out. But it was lonely, so lonely. She was tired of being alone. More important, she was tired of being without *him*.

Click was Click. Being close to him always shook up her insides. Seeing him shirtless had stirred her senses. But seeing their daughter's name, twined with hers, on his skin, had woken her heart. Somehow Click had managed to move on without pretending Amelia hadn't existed. She was with him every day. Tandy had no idea how to do that. But she wanted to. She wanted to think about her baby with peace. The only time Tandy had had peace in the last two years was when he'd held her close in that damn storm shelter.

Thinking of Amelia was still hard for her, too painful and raw. She couldn't think about her. Or what they'd been through. It brought her to her knees and tore her to pieces. She refused to be that weak—that vulnerable.

"Ta-dee?" Pearl lifted her little hands.

Tandy scooped her up. "Ready to go bye-bye?"

Pearl's eyes filled instantly with tears. "No bye-bye." She shook her head, her black curls bouncing.

"No..." She looked at Click then. "No bye-bye." She smiled.

"No bye-bye," Pearl agreed, burrowing against her. "No bye-bye." One small hand tangled in her long hair.

Click was watching, his brows drawn together.

Tandy shrugged. "She doesn't like that word. She cried

last time I said it, too." She paused. "I'm sorry, Pearl. Let's go."

Click patted Pearl's back. "Let's take Tandy for a ride."

"Da-gee?" Pearl asked. "Bashee?"

"Yep, Banshee is coming, too," he said.

Pearl nodded, sighed and rested her head on Tandy's shoulder.

"Where are we going?" he asked, leading her down the hall.

"The cabin," she said. "I need to see how salvageable it is. Or if I'm starting over. Again." The thought of moving into the ranch house held no appeal. But real estate in Fort Kyle was lean, to put it kindly.

"I'm no expert but…" he mumbled.

She nodded. "I know."

"But I'll take you," he said. "You been resting?"

It would have been easier to resist him if he wasn't so hell-bent on taking care of her. At the hospital, he'd stayed at her bedside, held her hand through her stitches and taken notes on what the doctor said.

She laughed, patting Pearl's back. "Yes, I've been resting. I feel like a slug. So does Banshee. He was about to scratch his way through the door this morning."

"He's too big a dog to stay cooped up." He held the front door open for them. "He's a damn good dog, Tandy."

"Remember what Scarlett said about being careful with your words?" She smiled. "He is a good dog. The best dog. Did I ever thank you for him?" she asked, a little distracted by the almost blue tones the sunlight picked up in his thick black hair.

He glanced at her, his smile heart-stoppingly beautiful. "You're welcome." He opened the door of a brand-new dark blue four-door truck and stepped back.

"Yours?" she asked, inspecting his ride with an appreciative eye. She nodded before leaning forward to strap Pearl into her car seat. Banshee jumped up and sat on the seat next to Pearl, earning him an adoring, "Bashee" from Pearl. "You keep Banshee company, okay, Pearl?" she said before climbing into Click's truck. "I like it," she said, running her hand along the interior. "New-car smell?" she said.

He nodded, assessing the truck with a critical eye. "First time I've ever ridden in a new truck, let alone owned one. But it's big enough for Pearl's seat and has a hauling package."

She studied him, hoping there was more to this purchase than just a new car. "When are you going trailer shopping?"

He grinned at her. "Soon, I guess. No rush." His eyes narrowed. "What about you?"

"What about me?" she asked.

"Scarlett tells me Doc Edwards's clinic is a mess." He drove out the Fire Gorge parking lot and onto the road.

She sighed. "I'm not beat yet. It'd help if he had equipment from this century." She shook her head. "I miss the vet hospital. Everything I needed was within reach. There was a sense of purpose and drive. I don't get that here. Half the time I feel like I'm the only one working. Even when Doc Edwards is there, he's not really *there*, you know?"

"So you're picking up the slack?" he asked.

"I'm not a DVM—there are some things I can't do." Not because she wasn't capable, but because she was a rule follower. "But I do what I can. And then some."

His smile faded. "Guess you're thinking about going back to Stonewall Crossing?"

"It's crossed my mind," she admitted.

"Gotta do what's right for you," he said, his knuckles whitening on the steering wheel.

"I'm not leaving anytime soon. Like I said, I'm not beat yet." She tried not to get hung up on his reaction.

Those blue-green eyes glanced her way, his posture easing. "Glad to hear it."

"Mew-sik," Pearl said from the back seat. "Peez."

Tandy's eyes went round. "Did you say please, Pearl?" She turned, staring at the grinning toddler in her seat. "Manners and brains."

"Peez peez," Pearl chanted.

Click chuckled, turning on the radio. Pearl started bouncing in her car seat and clapping her hands.

"She really loves mew-sik, doesn't she?" she asked him.

"I'm sure the lullabies help," he said.

She shook her head. "I doubt that."

"I don't," he argued. "She asks for music whenever I put her down. I try but last night she covered my mouth."

Tandy was too surprised to stop her laugh from bubbling up. "She did not."

"She did." His brow arched, the corner of his mouth kicking up. "I'm glad you think it's so funny." He looked younger when he smiled, like he wasn't carrying the weight of the world on his shoulders. And his laugh, rich and warm… She blew out a slow breath. He should laugh more. "Talk about dinging a man's ego."

She grabbed his forearm. "I'm sorry." But she kept laughing. Until his hand covered hers. If she was smart, she'd pull her hand away and shove the bubble of joy deep down inside. Except it was Click and his touch was magic. And deep down, she didn't want to pull away. She twined her fingers with his and smiled.

CLICK WAS A happy man. Sitting here on a blanket, Tandy at his side, watching Banshee and Pearl trail after the goats was as perfect a day as he could imagine.

"I was hoping it wasn't this bad," Tandy said, nodding at the pile of lumber that had been her home. "I'm not sure I can bear working for Doc Edwards all day and coming home to Uncle Woodrow every night." She sighed.

"Don't blame you," he said, trying to get the courage up to say what was on his mind.

"Guess I could look in town," she mumbled, plucking strands of grass absentmindedly. "Need to find a vehicle, too."

"Or you could stay here," he said, shooting for casual— he wasn't sure he succeeded.

Her hazel-green eyes met his. "What?"

"It's a big house, Tandy. Pearl and I are in one of five bedrooms. There's plenty of room." He cleared his throat. He could get lost in those eyes.

"Click, I can't… We can't…" She sputtered to a stop, stunned.

"Besides, Banshee's happy," He nodded at the dog trailing after the goats. "So is Pearl." He grinned, watching her trailing after Banshee. "You're already helping me out."

"People would talk," she said.

His brows rose. "And you'd care?"

She blew out a slow breath.

"Think on it," he said, pushing himself from the blanket to follow Pearl around the barn. He trusted Banshee, but there was no point tempting fate. The dog was tending the goats, someone needed to tend his daughter.

He hadn't expected Tandy to follow.

"She keeps you on your toes," Tandy said. "But it seems like you've found your groove."

He shook his head. "It does?" He chuckled. "Chalk it up to Pearl being so sweet-natured."

Pearl chose that moment to look their way. "Da da. Ta-dee," she said, waving. "Come."

"We're coming, cuddle bunny," he said. "Almost nap time."

"Ta-dee sing?" Pearl said.

"See?" He laughed, glancing at Tandy.

She had her hand over her mouth, trying to hold back the peals of laughter spilling from her lips. With the sun in her hair and her eyes alight with mischief, she'd never looked more beautiful. He stood, mesmerized by the vision she presented.

"Damn, woman, you take my breath away." He forced the words out.

Her laughter stopped, a look of pure surprise settling on her features.

"Ta-dee," Pearl said, holding out a flower. "Night-night?" she said, toddling toward them. "Ta-dee sing."

"Yes," Tandy said, kneeling and gathering her close. "I will sing you to sleep, cuddle bunny. Your daddy's acting silly anyway. Maybe he needs a nap, too."

"I'm good," he said, watching them walk into the house.

Banshee circled him, then sat at his side.

"Like the goats?" he asked the dog.

Banshee barked.

"Help me convince Tandy to stay and you can herd them all day long." He rubbed the dog's head.

It was a long shot, but a guy could hope. With Tandy, he seemed to have an endless supply of hope. He stared at the back door, but decided following her was a bad idea. Because if he went after her, he might push—and things were going too well to risk it.

"Let's check on the horses," he said to Banshee, walking the repaired fence line. The horses trotted up, saying hello to him and sniffing Banshee curiously. Banshee returned the favor. Click leaned against the fence, his eyes sweeping the property. He'd spent the last two days clearing any debris from the tornado. From metal stakes to clothing, he'd found all sorts of odds and ends. Domino and Blackjack had been spooked after the tornado, but no harm had been done and he wanted to keep it that way. He circled the entire corral before making his way back to the house.

Tandy was in the kitchen. "Making tea," she said. "Didn't see any in the fridge."

"Thanks," he said. "She go down okay?"

She nodded, her smile returning. "Guess it was the singing?"

He chuckled. "Low blow."

Banshee flopped onto the floor.

"You wore him out," she said, nodding at her dog.

"Pearl has that effect on people," he said, smiling as a soft snore rose from Banshee's place in the corner.

"Looks like the twister passed your place up." She put the glass jar in the windowsill, in the sunlight, so the tea could steep. "Amazing how my little place toppled and yours didn't get so much as a scratch."

"It did. One window," he said, washing his hands in the sink. "Had a bunch of odds and ends turn up, though."

"Oh, like what?" she asked, handing him the kitchen towel.

"A shoe. Some sort of hair…thing."

"Hair thing?" she asked, waiting.

"To curl your hair," he explained, loving the smile on her face.

"A curling iron?" she asked. "Here's hoping it wasn't in use when it got sucked up inside the funnel cloud."

He nodded. "That'd be unfortunate."

She grinned, rinsing out a baby bottle.

"You don't have to do that." He took the bottle from her, his hands closing over hers. She felt so good. "I didn't bring you here to clean up after Pearl and me."

She leaned against the counter, her gaze searching his. "I don't mind."

He stepped back, dropping the bottle back into the sink, and putting space between them. "Maybe I do. It wasn't that long ago you were bleeding all over me, remember?"

She smiled. "I guess I owe you an undershirt."

He shook his head. "You don't owe me a thing."

He hadn't planned on standing there, staring at her. But he did. And she stayed where she was, looking right back. The longer she stared at him, the harder it was to stay put. His fingers itched to touch her, his arms ached to hold her close...

"I'm happy you're doing this, Click," she said. "I think Lynnie would be thrilled to know she'd given you your dream."

He swallowed, nodding. "Almost."

Tandy's brow furrowed. "Almost?" She nodded. "I guess dreams change over time—"

"Mine hasn't. I still want what I always wanted." He took a step closer, his heart pounding.

"But... This is what you wanted," she said. "Your own place, training cutting horses, doing it your way—"

"With you," he said.

She blinked rapidly, her gaze falling from his. "Even now?" The question was a broken whisper.

He closed the distance between them but didn't touch her. "Always."

She looked up at him. "How? How can you look at me and not hurt? When…after… How do you get up, keep going and not ache?"

"I do, of course I do." His hand cradled her cheek. "Every day. She left a hole in my heart, one that'll never be filled. But looking at you…" He stepped closer. "Damn, Tandy, being away from you nearly broke me. Now, I look at you and miss what we had."

"We can't go back." She blinked, tears falling down her cheek.

His thumb wiped her tears away. "You'll never move forward if you keep holding on so tight. If you can't accept it wasn't your fault, then learn to forgive yourself. Our baby girl was stillborn, Tandy. You didn't cause that. I still cry, I still hurt, but I've made peace." He cleared his throat, fighting the tightness. "We both lost her. But you don't have to lose me, too. I'm here. And I still love you."

Tandy cradled his face between her hands, her thumb running across his lips. "You do?"

"I'll always love you," he said, clasping her hand and kissing her palm and the inside of her wrist.

She sucked in a deep, shuddering breath.

Click pulled her against him. "I wish I could take the pain away, Tandy, with all my heart."

She cried, gripping his shirt and pressing her mouth to his shoulder. His arms pressed her tight, knowing she needed this but hating the depths of her grief. She sobbed, her arms twining about his waist, gripping his belt for support.

"I got you," he said, burying his face in her hair. "I won't let you go." He scooped her up and carried her into the front parlor. He sat cradling her close, rocking her, until she'd cried herself dry.

Chapter Twelve

Tandy woke with a terrible headache. Not just her head, but her eyes and throat. She stared up at the ceiling overhead, but it was too dark to make much out. She rolled over, staring at the massive window with the white lace curtains. From the thick black sky outside, Tandy knew she'd slept the day away. And now, she was wide awake.

It had been a long time since Tandy had felt this alert. She was exhausted, her body drained to the point of inertia, but she was awake. The numbness she'd been clinging to was gone. Every nerve felt exposed, raw and hyperaware.

She ran a hand over her face and pushed off the bed.

Her stomach growled, reminding her she'd skipped lunch to avoid more chitchat with her uncle. She didn't know how her cousins put up with him. She'd yet to make it through a meal when a simple conversation hadn't unleashed some sort of booming diatribe from the great Woodrow Boone. His opinion, of course, was always the right one. So attempting to challenge or question his topic of conversation or opinion only increased the likelihood they'd talk about whatever it was for even longer. Tandy had given up after her first dinner there.

Would her uncle be railing about her absence at the dinner table?

Click wouldn't mind her raiding his fridge.

The door creaked on its hinges. Tandy waited, but no one came down the hall so she slipped out. Banshee was sprawled across the parlor, snoring softly.

Click had left a light on in the kitchen, so she could see easily.

The first thing she saw was Click, sound asleep in the rocking chair.

She stared at him, frozen in place. He wore work-worn jeans and a white undershirt that clung to every ridge and curve of his chest. All brawn and muscle and beauty. She smiled at the ink that peeked out from under the left sleeve.

She'd wanted to believe the doctor, wanted to believe she hadn't done something to cause Amelia's death. But her mother said he was being kind, to ease her guilt. And she *had* felt guilty, so damn guilty. Thinking of Amelia was too hard. She had no right to tears or sorrow when it was her fault. It was Toben who rescued her from their mother, dragging her with him before the crush of guilt had almost killed her. No matter how hard he tried to get through to her, Tandy refused to hear him. It hurt too much to grieve, to face what she'd done.

Click's words cut her loose the way no one else could. Amelia had been his, too. The pain was there, but it was different now. It would take time to accept it was okay to miss her, to grieve for her, and not blame herself. That hadn't been an option before. Whether her mother realized the damage her words had done to her, Tandy did—now.

As much as it had hurt to see Pearl, to know what it meant he'd done, she couldn't hold it against him. He'd been just as lost as she was—searching for some way to find a purpose. And they had Pearl now. Sweet, happy Pearl.

So much pain. So much time lost.

The only hurt she couldn't quite make peace with was the hurt she'd caused Click.

"Tandy?" His voice was a low rumble, thick with sleep.

"I'm sorry," she whispered. Her stomach growled loudly, rousing Banshee from his place on the floor.

"Hungry?" Click chuckled.

"What makes you say that?" she asked, still whispering. Her stomach roared again.

He pointed at her. "When did you eat last?"

She shrugged. "I had some toast this morning." She searched the walls for some sign of a clock. "What time is it?"

"Almost midnight," he said, pushing out the rocking chair.

She stared up at him, his face shadowed. "You go on to bed—"

"Why are we whispering?" he asked.

She smiled. "Habit?" She looked down the hallway. "Lynnie never liked us up after she went to bed."

He grinned. "She did not. I think she knew what we were up to."

Tandy's body tingled. "You do?" How many hot summer nights had she and Click slipped from their rooms—she from her uncle's place and he from Lynnie's. They'd meet up, toting flashlights and wearing pajamas and boots. In the beginning it had been innocent. Long walks under the starry sky and holding hands with sweaty palms. But that last summer, she and Click started a fire that burned hot for years.

"I do," he said, so close his breath brushed her forehead. "She said we were a good match. Two broken birds that, together, flew straight."

Tandy wished the lights were on then, so she could see his face and search his eyes. Her stomach growled again.

Click chuckled. "Let's get something in that belly of yours before you wake Pearl up."

She followed Click into the kitchen, blinking against the sudden light from the overhead fan.

"What did you eat?" she asked, pulling open the refrigerator and peering inside. "Is this all you have?"

"I don't cook much. Pearl still eats mostly baby food and fruit." He ran a hand over his face.

She pulled the basket of eggs out. "Is this ham safe?" she asked.

He nodded.

"Ham and eggs it is," she said. She cooked, comfortable in Lynnie's kitchen, while Click set the table. They didn't say much, but it wasn't awkward. It was natural. She put ham, eggs and toast on two plates and carried them to the table.

"Looks good," he said, digging in.

She watched him, smiling as he cleaned his plate with enthusiasm. "I guess I wasn't the only hungry one?"

He grinned. It was one hell of a grin, all dimples and yummy creases.

She cleared her throat. "Why weren't you sleeping in your bed?" she asked between bites.

"Thought you might get up," he said, leaning back in his chair, one long leg extending out from under the table.

Sitting here just the two of them, it was hard to miss just how much space he filled. Or maybe it only felt that way. The longer those blue eyes watched her, the smaller the room became. And hotter. She was growing warmer by the minute. "You waited up for me?" she asked.

He shrugged.

"You knew I'd cook you something," she teased, needing to ease the mounting tension between them.

"I wanted to make sure you were okay. Seems like every time we're alone together I make you cry." His fingers tapped the linoleum tabletop. "I'm sorry."

She set her fork down, searching for the right words. "Momma said crying's weak. But it turned out she said a lot of things that were wrong. I was too fragile to see it. It took hearing the truth from someone who's never lied to me to make me realize that." She sat forward, reaching across the table for his hand. "Don't be sorry for today. Please."

He nodded, the muscle in his jaw working.

"I'm the one who should be sorry," she said. "I pushed you away when you were hurting, too."

He stood, tugging her from her chair. "I should have dug in and stayed."

"You wouldn't do that, Click. You've always done what I wanted, what you thought would make me happy. Even then," she finished. Her heart, just as awake as the rest of her, thumped heavily in her chest. She was done asking why he had this effect on her. Their connection was just as unwavering as it had always been. She craved him—craved the way he made her feel.

"What would make you happy now, Tandy?" The words were gruff and raw, resonating up her spine.

She stood on tiptoe, holding on to his shoulders for balance, and pressed her lips to his.

HER LIPS FELT like heaven. Gentle, slow, tentative, her kiss bowled him over. It was the last thing he'd expected. Wanted, yes, more than anything. But now? She'd cried for more than an hour, so worn out she'd passed out cold against him.

He wanted to believe that this was about them, about her needing and wanting him. "Tandy." He placed a hand, lightly, on her chest. "Are you kissing me because you want to kiss *me*? Or because you're lonely and you know I won't say no?"

"I've never separated one from the other," she said, staring into his eyes. "I'm lonely because I've been missing you." Her eyes searched his. "Yes, I want to kiss you. If…if you want—"

He groaned, his mouth sealing to hers with a hunger that startled him. There was no *if* when it came to wanting Tandy. He'd wake from dreams, remembering her scent and the silk of her curves, and damn near rip his pillow apart. She was real, in his arms, offering her lips to him. If this was what she wanted, he'd happily oblige. It had been too long since he'd tasted her.

Her fingers tangled in his hair. She arched into him, her breasts pressing against his chest, soft and full. He groaned, his hands sliding down her back—then up. He wanted to hold her to him, he wanted to touch every inch.

The tip of her tongue touched his, and he all but slid to the floor. His hands fisted in the fabric of her top as his tongue delved into the warmth of her mouth.

It was her turn to moan. Damn but he loved the sound of it. Even after all this time, he did this to her. His lips moved over hers, each kiss more frantic than the last. When one stopped and the next began, he didn't know.

He was vaguely aware of Pearl, the squeak and rustle over the baby monitor. Some nights she woke, fussing and fretful, until he soothed her back to sleep. But if she got too worked up, he'd be pacing the floor with her for hours.

"Pearl," he said, tearing his lips from hers.

"I'll go," she answered, her breath labored. "Maybe she'll drift off with a song."

He pressed a kiss to her nose. "All you."

She smiled up at him, her fingers stroking his mouth before she left him standing in the middle of the kitchen.

"Shh, pretty Pearl." Tandy's voice came through the monitor. "Sleep sweet little one," she murmured. She hummed softly, the raspy timbre holding him captive. He closed his eyes, listening as she sang the only lullaby Lynnie knew.

"Baby, Baby, don't you cry
Hush and hear my lullaby
Rest your head and close your eyes
Let me rock you into dreams
Baby, Baby, don't you cry
Hush and hear my lullaby."

Click smiled, quietly carrying the dishes to the sink while Tandy sang the lullaby again. He was humming, too, warmed by the love and safety those lines stirred within him. He'd have to remember it next time, in case Tandy wasn't here to sing for Pearl.

He was still humming when he finished washing the skillet Tandy had used to cook their dinner. He wiped his hands on the kitchen towel and turned to find Tandy in the doorway, watching him.

"You have a nice voice," she said.

"Not as nice as yours," he argued, leaning against the kitchen counter. "Thanks for that. She seems more comfortable with you than she is with me."

She shook her head. "You feel calmer when she's with me." She smiled. "Babies sense that."

She was right. He was still uncertain with Pearl. Every

day was a little easier, but being a father was hardly second nature. Yet. "I'm trying."

"I know. She knows. It's plain to see she loves you."

"I love her," he murmured. When or how it happened, he wasn't sure. It could have been the first time she'd turned those big eyes on him and smiled. It could have been her giggle. Or the way she said Da da. Maybe it was the combination of all bits and pieces of the time they'd spent together. He loved his baby girl more than he'd imagined was possible. "Even if I don't know what I'm doing."

"Tired?" she asked, her gaze lingering on his face—and his lips.

He stared at her, the feel of her lips still singeing his.

"You should get some sleep," she said.

He arched a brow. She kept looking at him like that and he'd never get any sleep. "You going to bed?" It was probably for the best. His hunger for her was powerful. Kissing was one thing.

She stared at him, swallowing before she said, "Are we?"

Her voice was soft, but he heard the "we" easily enough. He blew out a slow breath, her words all too appealing. There was no denying he wanted her. But not yet. "Tandy—"

"To sleep. Next to you." Her cheeks flamed red. "Just sleep. Or not. I… I can go to my room." She all but ran from the kitchen.

Click stayed where he was, gripping the kitchen counter, staring at the empty doorway, telling himself over and over that he wouldn't follow her. Today had changed things between them; he felt it deep down. But that didn't mean he was going to hop in her bed and love her the way he'd spent so many damn nights thinking about.

He bit out a curse and turned off all the lights before heading to the bathroom. He paused, glancing at her door, then closed the bathroom door behind him. His evening routine was the same: shower, brush his teeth, tug on boxer shorts and head to the room he shared with Pearl. But once he was lying there, his brain refused to turn off. She was on the other side of the wall, wanting him at her side. To sleep. Nothing more. How the hell was he going to sleep? He rolled over, punched the pillow into shape then turned the other way. He sat up and ran a hand through his hair. *I'm a damn fool.*

He peered into Pearl's bed, pulling the blanket up, and stood.

He went into the kitchen, unplugged Pearl's monitor and headed into Tandy's room. She was reading, the bedside lamp on, but she didn't say a word as he swept into her room and plugged in the monitor. He looked at her then, stunned by the smile on her face.

He shook his head, completely whipped.

She closed the book and set it on the bedside table, flipping back the blankets on his side of the bed in invitation.

He hesitated, torn between the right thing and giving her what she wanted. She patted the mattress once, and he caved. The sight of one creamy thigh had him biting back a groan. "What are you wearing?" he growled, sliding between the sheets and lying back against the pillows. His body was rock hard and throbbing. He was beginning to rethink this.

"Enough," she said, sliding close enough to rest her head on his chest. "I like your boxers."

He chuckled and turned off the light. "Wore them just for you," he teased.

She sighed, burrowing closer, the silk of her hair

draping across his shoulder. He closed his eyes, wrapping an arm around her. His hand rested on her hip, the edge of her lace-trimmed undies forcing him to move his hand up. But the feel of her satin-soft skin wasn't much better. He flexed his hand, his body more than willing to take things further. She wriggled closer, fitting her curves tightly against him, before easing into sleep. He wouldn't have it any other way. It was torture, but he'd suffer through it.

Chapter Thirteen

Tandy measured out the pancake mix and dumped it into the bowl. She smiled at Pearl, sitting among a pile of plastic bowls on the floor, and started whisking the ingredients together. She'd woken up to Pearl's sweet gibber-jabber over the monitor. As hard as it was to leave Click sleeping, she figured he could use a break.

Pearl's delighted "Ta dee" had been the best good-morning she'd ever heard. All through her diaper change, Pearl had babbled and smiled with such happiness that Tandy had no choice but to be cheerful, too.

That was exactly how she felt. "Cheerful," she said to Pearl. "You wanna help me cook, Pearl?"

Pearl smiled up at her and whacked one of the plastic bowls with the rubber spatula Tandy had given her. She giggled at the sound it made, repeating it again and again.

"Like that?" Tandy said, giggling right along with her.

Coffee was brewing. Click liked his black. She preferred a little milk and sugar, but they were both running low.

"Once we're done cooking, we need to go shopping," Tandy said. "The cupboard's almost empty."

There was plenty of baby food, but not much else. Pearl might do just fine on mashed sweet potatoes and ham, strained peas and blended beef. But Click needed something a little less...pureed.

"Go go go," Pearl chanted.

"Yes, we can go together," she said, glad it was Sunday. "No work for me." She peered out the window at the yard. Banshee sat, regarding the herd of goats. "We'll need to get Banshee something to eat, too." If she could get Click's help, she wanted to sift through the cabin's wreckage and see what might be rescued.

She poured some batter on the griddle, the sizzle telling her it was just the right temperature. Her stomach growled.

"Yum-yum?" Pearl asked.

"Yes, ma'am. Cooking some yum-yum for you and me and Daddy. Then we'll go see what we can find," she told Pearl, glancing at her cabin again. If she were lucky, she might find some clothes. And her favorite pair of boots. Poor Banshee loved his bed. If the wind hadn't carried them away, maybe she could bring them here. If this was where she was planning on staying. With Pearl. And Click.

She stared at the pancake batter, the edges searing golden brown.

This morning, the sun had spilled into her bedroom and she'd stayed perfectly still. Not because of the sunrise or the majestic view out her window. No, it was because Click held her. His hand rested against her belly, his long fingers splayed wide. His head rested by hers, his steady breathing brushing her ear. There was no room between his chest and her back. He'd pulled her tight and pinned her close. Exactly where she'd wanted to be.

If Pearl hadn't stirred, she'd still be there.

"Mew-sik, Ta-dee?" Pearl asked.

"You want to sing?" she asked. "After I finish cooking, I'll show you my guitar—" But her guitar was in the cabin. "I'll play the piano for you." She scooped the pancakes off the griddle and poured four more on.

"Sing?" Pearl asked, humming. "Peez?"

When she'd found out she was expecting, Tandy had written a dozen songs to sing to her baby. Mostly lullabies, meant for quiet moments. But not all of them. It had been a long time since she'd sung them, but now, smiling into Pearl's eager eyes, she wanted to sing them.

"My baby likes pie, sweet cherries and cream. It tickles her tummy and tastes like a dream." She rubbed her tummy, making Pearl smile. "My baby likes pie, apple tart and green. Sticky on her fingers, she licks them all clean." She pretended to lick her fingers. This time Pearl giggled. Tandy winked, flipping the pancakes before continuing.

"My baby likes pie, berry red and black. Sugary goodness, keeps bringing her back." She stooped and hugged Pearl, earning her a kiss. "My baby likes pie, pumpkin gold and spice. With a dollop of whipped cream it sure tastes nice." She touched Pearl's nose. Pearl touched Tandy's nose. "I better get the pancakes off the griddle or they'll burn, pretty Pearl. Okay?"

Pearl nodded.

"You sure are an agreeable little thing," Tandy said. "Anyone ever told you that?"

Pearl nodded, her gaze fixed on Tandy's face.

"I thought so. You make my heart smile, little cuddle bunny." She bent down. "You know that?"

Pearl hugged her again. "Ta-dee."

"A serenade, pancakes and the prettiest ladies in the great state of Texas," Click said, shaking his head. "I don't know how I ever got so lucky."

"Hi, Dada," Pearl said, waving her spatula at him. "Spoon. Ta-dee cook."

Click nodded. "Yes, ma'am. You and Tandy are cooking. Smells good."

Pearl nodded. "Yum." She pointed at Tandy. "Ta-dee sing."

"I like her songs, too." Click's gaze settled on her then. She'd never figured out how a simple look could get her so worked up. He'd always been able to do that—make her stomach flip and her heart beat a little too fast. Like now. "Not much I don't like about her."

"Breakfast is almost ready." She focused on the pancakes. "You're short some bacon or sausage. And you're out of eggs. Pearl and I've been talking about going to the store. You can come, too, if you want. You don't even have any potatoes or I'd have fried some up—"

He was behind her, his breath tickling her ear. "Looks perfect to me. Thank you."

She shivered, smiling. "You're welcome."

"Sleep okay?" he asked, his hand sliding across her stomach and setting her nerves on fire.

She nodded, too breathless to say much. "You?"

"Yes, ma'am," he said, dropping a soft kiss right below her ear. "You smell so good, Tandy." He breathed her in, making her toes curl.

"Dada kiz Ta-dee?" Pearl said, tugging on Click's jeans. "Dada kiz?"

He scooped her up and dropped kisses all over her face, making her squeal and giggle.

"Ta-dee kiz?" she asked, leaning toward Tandy.

Tandy wasn't about to say no. She grabbed Pearl to her, pressing kisses on each soft cheek and her smiling mouth, making a big smacking sound for effect.

Pearl was laughing then, her little arms around Tandy's

neck. It felt good. It felt right. And it suddenly scared her. Tandy shifted Pearl onto her hip, swallowing back the unexpected emotion tightening her throat. "You want to flip the last pancake, Pearl?"

Pearl nodded, watching as Tandy showed her how to flip it. Pearl tried, but the pancake ended up on the floor. Her smile drooped.

"That's Banshee's breakfast," she said. "Let's call him in to eat." She put Pearl down and let her toddle over to the back door.

"Da-gee! Ba-shee! Come," Pearl called, clapping her hands.

Banshee came, barreling across the yard and straight for Pearl. He slammed on the brakes right before he slid into her. He sat, let the little girl hug him, then licked her right across the face.

"Damn good dog," Click whispered.

Tandy glanced over her shoulder at him, struck once more by just how fine he was. When he smiled at her, nodding at Banshee and Pearl, she had no choice but to smile back.

"Da-gee ki," Pearl squealed, laughing.

"Big, wet, doggie kisses," Tandy agreed, pulling dishes from the cabinet and setting the table. "He gives you kisses because he loves you."

"Can I help?" Click asked.

"Any syrup?" She smiled up at him, surprised by her nervousness.

"I doubt it, but I'll check." He pulled open the pantry, put his hands on his hips and shook his head. "Looks like we'll be going into town after breakfast."

"Go go go," Pearl said.

GROWING UP THE way he had, Click didn't have high expectations. Experience had taught him that good things always came to a hard, sudden stop and talk was worthless. His dad made promises he never kept and his mother found ways to excuse the man every time. After a while, Click understood a promise was a lie and trust an illusion. The idea of a family—loyal and devoted, unconditional love—was a bad joke. Lynnie had been the only exception. Until Tandy.

He'd never imagined someone would love him the way Tandy had. In her eyes, he was everything. Her confidence in him was unshakeable. With her, he'd believed life could be more. Life could be good. And family, through highs and lows, was possible. They'd been through some damn-near bottomless lows, but here they were.

In a grocery store. Shopping. Together.

Watching Tandy read the ingredients on a cereal box, her hand stroking over Pearl's silky black curls, made him happy.

"Dada?" Pearl asked, patting his hand on the shopping cart handle.

He smiled at her. "Yes, baby girl?"

She smiled. "Dada." Her hand stayed on his.

He dropped a kiss on her forehead. "Yes, ma'am."

"I think this is the best option," Tandy said, holding a cereal box in each hand.

"Which one?" he asked, trying not to smile as he picked up a box of brightly colored rings. "Why not this?"

She glanced at the box and frowned at him. "For Pearl? It's nothing but sugar. You don't want…" She stopped at his smile. "You're teasing me?"

He chuckled. "A bit."

She shook her head and dropped the cereal she'd picked out into the basket. "You think you're cute."

"You do," he said.

She shot him a look, but the flush of her cheeks was reward enough. He pushed the cart, fully aware that the good folks of Fort Kyle were interested in their shopping trip. That, or they were all smitten with Pearl.

Tandy seemed to be on a mission, filling the cart with things he didn't know he'd ever need. If she thought they needed it, who was he to argue?

When he pushed the cart into the checkout lane, he saw Scarlett walk in. She was on her cell phone, listening more than talking. But once she spotted them, she hung up and headed straight for them.

"Hi," she said, hugging them. "Looks like you're stocking up. Thanks for texting me, Click, so I didn't worry over her."

"Sorry," Tandy said. "I sort of fell asleep. It was midnight when I woke up."

Click smiled, unloading the groceries onto the conveyor belt. Tandy might not have realized what she'd just said, but there was plenty of room for interpretation. The look on their older cashier's face told him exactly how she interpreted it—and she didn't approve.

"Oh." Scarlett glanced back and forth between them. "I was picking up some watermelons for the ranch and then I was heading your way. I figure you'd need a ride back to the ranch house."

Click looked at Tandy, the same time Tandy looked at him.

"Click was going to help me at the cabin," Tandy said. "If there's anything worth saving."

He nodded. "Sure."

"Okay. I can help," Scarlett said. "But I wouldn't hold your breath."

Click agreed. He didn't want them digging around until he was sure there was no danger. A storm like that could cause all sorts of structural and electrical problems. Not to mention the wildlife rousted up. He didn't want Banshee getting sprayed by a skunk hiding out. Or have a run-in with the javelinas he'd seen tearing through the back fields a few times now. Best to leave them alone.

"Your father planning on sending over a tractor or truck anytime soon?" Click asked, paying for the groceries and steering the cart toward the door.

Scarlett shook her head, looking thoughtful. "He hasn't mentioned it. To be honest, he seemed downright pleased that you didn't come home last night, Tandy."

Why would Woodrow Boone be happy she'd stayed with him? It didn't make much sense.

"But he did want me to invite you and Pearl out for dinner," Scarlett said.

"What's he up to?" Tandy asked.

Scarlett shrugged. "I've given up trying to figure him out."

"Da da," Pearl said, yawning.

"Nap time?" Scarlett asked.

He nodded. "I'd feel better if we hold off rooting through the cabin, until I can make sure it's safe. If that's okay?"

Tandy frowned.

"Better safe than sorry," he murmured.

She nodded. "I'll just wash these again." She glanced at her clothing.

"My washing machine works just fine," he said.

"Then I'll see ya'll for dinner?" Scarlett asked. "Unless you want to come with me now?" She glanced back and forth between them.

Tandy glanced at him, her cheeks going red. "Do you mind taking me later?" she asked.

He grinned, shaking his head.

"I can sing to Pearl," Tandy said. "She likes it when I sing to her. Don't you, Pearl?"

"Ta-dee sing." Pearl nodded, reaching for her. "Sing sing."

Scarlett smiled. "Well, then. I'll see you later. Watermelon for dessert." She winked and left them.

Tandy stared after her cousin. "I should probably go with her."

"Is that what you want?" he asked, unloading the groceries into the back of the truck.

Her eyes were light mossy green in the afternoon Texas sun, boring into his and holding him captive. She drew in an unsteady breath. "You ready to go, Pearl?" she asked. Her gaze falling from his.

He could breathe then. She wanted to stay with them. And damn if he wasn't smiling from ear to ear.

"Go go," Pearl said, reaching for Tandy. "Dashee?"

"He's waiting at home," Tandy said, opening the back door and buckling Pearl into the truck. "We'll go see Banshee now. Then go night-night." She yawned.

"You holding up okay?" he asked. "When do you go back to the doctor to have your stitches checked out?"

She shrugged. "Next week." Her eyes searched his as she climbed into the passenger seat. "Stop worrying about me."

He shook his head, closing the passenger door behind her.

Tandy and Pearl sang most of the way home. When they weren't singing, they carried on a sort of one-sided conversation that Tandy managed to understand—sort of. He had no idea what his daughter was saying, but they were giggling and it was hard to ask too many questions. When they got there, Pearl wanted Tandy.

"I know, I know," he said. "Tandy sing."

Pearl smiled, so did Tandy.

"Go on," he said, unloading the groceries.

He put the groceries away, the sound of Tandy's sweet voice floating down the hallway. He poured himself a glass of the tea she'd made earlier and stared out the kitchen window. In the distance, he saw Lynnie's goats. Correction, his goats were lazily eating their way across the tall grass.

He needed to put in some sheep and goat wire before the herd wandered onto the Boone property. He knew Tandy wouldn't have minded a little goat-powered lawn-mowing service. Woodrow Boone was another matter altogether.

He paused, mulling over the motivation for tonight's dinner invitation. What would his neighbor do if he knew Click wasn't ready to sell? Not now. Maybe never.

If he let his dream take root, followed it through to the end, he might never leave this place. Sitting in a rocker on the porch, he'd sketched out some rough plans—laid it out until he could see every pen and stall, chute and walker wheel.

He'd need to build a bunkhouse and hire on a few hands, no more than five, to keep the place running smoothly. He'd want good people, hardworking and horse-loving. When he trained, he spared the whip and the spur. It had never been about dominating an animal. It was learning the best way to communicate with them. Respect was key—

"Click?" Tandy stood at his side. "You're lost in thought. Making big plans for the place?"

He smiled down at her. "Just thinking."

She shook her head. "Thinking? What's stopping you, Click?" She rested a hip on the counter. "As Lynnie would say, time's a'wastin'." She paused. "Or how about, 'You're not getting any younger'?"

"You trying to tell me something?" he asked, running a long strand of her hair between his thumb and forefinger. So soft.

"Yes," she murmured. "Do it. She wanted you to."

He turned, focusing 100 percent of his attention on her. He cupped her cheek in his hand, his thumb smoothing her brow and running the ridge of her nose. The curve of her cheek was smooth. The swell of her lip, inviting.

Not yet. Not until he knew she was ready. He wasn't going to take chances with her heart. Or his.

He swallowed, dropped a kiss to her forehead and stepped back. "I'm gonna ride out, survey the fence line." The flash of surprise on her face almost made him rethink his objections. Almost.

Chapter Fourteen

Tandy was pulling the banana muffins from the oven when the house phone started to ring. She set the tray on the counter, pushed the stove shut with her heel and answered the phone.

"Hello?" she answered.

"Who's this?" the voice asked.

"Tandy Boone," she answered. "And this?"

"It's Miss Francis, dear. What a pleasant surprise, hearing your voice." The old lady chuckled. "Click offered to drive me to Alpine, and I wanted to make sure he was still available."

"I'm sorry, Miss Francis, he's out working. But I'll make sure he calls you just as soon as he comes inside." She jotted a note on the small tablet thumbtacked to the wall. "When were you planning on going into town?"

"Tomorrow afternoon. Monday traffic isn't too bad." Miss Francis paused. "You can come, too, if you'd like. I heard about the cabin. Bet you'll be needing a few things?"

She chewed on the end of the pencil. Shopping someplace other than Fort Kyle's Ranch and Farm supplies would be nice. Sure, they had plenty of jeans to choose from. But that was about it. "I'll have to see if I can take the afternoon off, Miss Francis. But I appreciate you including me."

"Of course, dear, of course." She chuckled. "I can't tell you how pleased I am to hear your voice."

Tandy smiled. "You are?"

"Of course I am. That boy deserves some happiness. Seems to me, you're that for him. You tell him to call me now, you hear?"

"Yes, ma'am," she answered.

"Good girl. See you tomorrow."

Tandy hung up the phone, staring at the yellow handset mounted to the wall. Banshee pushed her hand. "What?" she asked, smiling at the dog. "You can't have a muffin, Banshee. It'll make your stomach upset." She ran a hand over his broad head. "But I did get you a treat." She crossed the room, pulling the large box of dog biscuits from the pantry.

The phone rang again, making her spin and trip over Banshee.

She was laughing and breathless when she answered the phone. "Miss Francis?"

"No," a voice said. "I'm looking for Aaron Hale."

Tandy frowned. "Click?" she asked.

"Yes, Click. Is he available?" the woman asked. "I need to speak with him."

Tandy picked up the pencil. "He's out working. Can I take a message for him?"

There was a long pause. "My name is Georgia Miles. I wanted to speak with him."

Tandy's heart thudded to a stop. Georgia. Pearl's mom.

"Is that possible?" Georgia asked. "He can't call me back, and I won't be able to call again for a while."

Tandy snapped out of it. "Let me see if I can flag him down. Can you wait a minute?"

"I'll wait."

Tandy hurried out the back door, shielding her eyes. No sign of him. She ran to the barn, calling for him. "Click?" She turned back when he rode into the yard. "You've got a phone call. Important."

He frowned. "Important?"

"Pearl's mom," she managed. "I can take Domino. You should get it."

He swung out of the saddle, his nod tight as he pressed the reins into her hand. He headed into the house, his posture growing more rigid with each step. Her heart hurt for him. And Pearl. Was there some sort of understanding between Click and the woman? What would happen to Pearl once Georgia was done with her treatment? Would Click lose her?

The pressure was sudden, compressing her chest— emptying her lungs and squeezing her heart. She watched him disappear into the house with dread seeping into her bones.

Tandy led Domino into the barn. She removed the saddle and saddle blanket, hanging them on the rack mounted to the wall. The whole time, she was thinking of Click. It wasn't fair. He and Pearl just found the rhythm. Would Georgia take his daughter?

Click would do whatever it took to keep her. Wouldn't he?

There was a chance she'd lose them. Click. And Pearl.

She finished brushing Domino and turned the horse into the small paddock behind the barn. She lingered, wanting to give Click some privacy. But, when he didn't come back, she gave up and headed back to the kitchen.

He wasn't in the kitchen.

Or the parlor.

Or the bedroom.

Was everything okay?

She was headed back to her room when the bathroom door opened and he stepped out. His thick black hair was wet, like the towel wrapped low around his waist. She did her best not to stare. She'd seen him shirtless before, countless times. And, somehow, the sight never failed to make her desperate with want.

"I... You okay?" she asked, rattled. "Never mind. Not now." She stepped back.

His blue-green gaze pinned hers, on fire for her.

"I... I..." She closed the distance between them, mindless as she slid her arms around his neck and pressed herself against him—driving him into the wall at his back. She wanted to comfort him, yes. But she also wanted him. So much she ached.

He caught her, his arms viselike around her.

His skin was warm beneath her hands. The ball of his shoulders, the clenched thickness of his upper arms, he was strong yet gentle. His breath powered out of him as his mouth sealed against hers. She moaned, her fingers threading through his hair and tightening, holding him close.

His lips parted, the slide of his tongue against hers making her knees buckle. But his arms were around her, pressing her against him and holding her up.

Her hands stroked over his chest, her fingers exploring the planes and edges of his sides and stomach. He was all muscle, honed from working hard. His hands, calloused and strong, tugged her shirt from her jeans and slid beneath her shirt. Her skin contracted, every nerve humming with frantic need. She wanted him so much. His hands, his mouth, his body.

His hand moved up her spine, slipping beneath her bra strap.

Tandy's fingers moved quickly, freeing the buttons and shrugging out of her cotton shirt.

He slid a bra strap from her shoulder and bent to press a kiss to her shoulder. A moan tore from his throat as his hands freed the clasp of her bra.

"Da-gee, Da-gee," Pearl sang. "Sing sing Da-gee."

Click froze. "No," he groaned softly, burying his face against her throat.

She blew out a shaky breath, her body trembling. No was right. She craved this, hungered for him. It had been so long. Her need was all-consuming. His hands brushed down her sides, teasing her tightly strung nerves.

His gaze swept over her face, lingering on her parted lips.

She shook her head, his hunger pulling her back in. "Stop."

"I can't," he said, tracing her lower lip. He leaned forward, his openmouthed kiss too good.

"Da-gee da-gee Ba-shee," Pearl sang. "Da da, Da da."

Tandy stepped away from him, crossing her arms over her chest and holding her bra in place. "I'll get her," she said, staring at his towel. "You might want another shower. A cold one."

There was something incredibly satisfying about his state of arousal. He wanted her. Seeing that look on his face, the way he struggled with self-control, was empowering and humbling. "Click?" she whispered.

"Going," he said. And with a shake of his head, he headed back into the bathroom. She smiled as the shower came on. Once she was dressed, she opened the bedroom door and smiled at Pearl.

"Ta-dee, Ta-dee, Ta-dee," Pearl sang happily. "Hi."

"Hi," she answered. "Sleep well, snuggle bunny?" she

asked. She scooped her out of her crib, changed her diaper and followed her down the hallway into the parlor.

"Da da?" Pearl asked.

"In the shower," she said, smiling. "Thirsty? Want a drink?"

Pearl nodded. "Peez."

Tandy headed into the kitchen for a sippy cup. The notepad was on the kitchen table, so Tandy carried it back to its place by the phone. But Click's note made her pause. She swallowed, the bold script making the words ominous.

A name—Georgia Miles—and a phone number.

Below it, he'd written Kevin Glenn and a question. Does he handle custody cases?

CLICK WATCHED HIS daughter make the rounds. She'd started with Tandy, chattering away with her and Scarlett. When she took a board book to Evelyn Boone and climbed into her lap, he could tell she'd won the woman over. His daughter called her Ev and kissed her on the cheek, thanking the woman for reading to her. While Click couldn't help feeling suspicious of the woman, he was willing to reconsider his original assessment—for Pearl.

Pearl. His daughter. Her sweet, easy nature was impossible to ignore. She was special, something to protect. Something worth fighting for, if it came down to it. His phone call with Georgia had been brief, timed, but it had rocked him to the core. He'd sort of hoped she'd disappeared. Turns out, she was planning to come see them.

"She's quite the charmer," Woodrow Boone said, accepting the coffee Scarlett was handing out. "My grandson Cal is the same. Smart, too—maybe too smart for a boy his age. Boy should get out more, scrape his knees and get his hands dirty now and then."

"Dad." Scarlett frowned. "Be nice."

Woodrow took a sip of his coffee and frowned right back at her. "I'm stating a fact. Not being mean."

Scarlett shrugged and returned to her spot by Tandy on the floor, one of Pearl's puzzles spread out on the throw rug. It was almost normal, almost like a family... Except for the way Woodrow Boone had been watching him all night. The older man was sizing him up, plain and simple. The only exception had been when Pearl was involved. Woodrow, like his wife, was smitten with his little daughter.

"Who does Cal belong to?" he asked, hoping to keep conversation somewhat neutral. Click had spent some time with the rest of Woodrow's children, but Scarlett was the only one he was close to.

"Cal is India's boy. Don't know if you remember my son Deacon?" He shook his head. "He's been helping my brother Teddy out a bit, in Stonewall Crossing. He lost his two daughters and his wife. Eighteen-wheeler accident. Damn driver was on drugs." The grief on the older man's face was masked quickly. "I keep telling Deacon to move on. Kelsey, his dear departed wife, wouldn't want him moping and being alone. She was a spitfire, that one."

Click couldn't think of a thing to say to that. Woodrow Boone would probably be a lot like his sister—Tandy's mother—Susan when it came to doling out advice and support to their kids. But, to give Woodrow some credit, he lacked the bitterness that hardened his sister. Susan Boone was a piece of work, in a class by herself. He didn't know what made the older woman that way, and he stopped caring when her sour moods and judgmental opinions hurt

Tandy. Where Susan was intentional, Woodrow was just clueless. "I'm sorry for your loss."

Woodrow looked at him then, his eyes narrowing ever so slightly. "Part of life, it seems. Losing folks you care about. Your aunt was a good woman."

He nodded.

"Da da?" Pearl said, smiling at him. "Music?"

"Music?" he asked, glancing Tandy's way. He loved his daughter, but there was no way he was going to humiliate himself.

"Peez," she said, shooting Woodrow Boone a shy smile.

"Well, now, that's too pretty a request to deny," Woodrow said. "Tandy? Go get a guitar and play something for this little sweet pea."

"Ta-dee sing," Pearl said to Woodrow.

"You like Tandy's singing?"

Pearl nodded, her shiny black curls bouncing.

"Wanna help me, Pearl?" Tandy asked, holding out her hand. Pearl was quick to take it and follow her out.

"She has the voice of an angel," Woodrow said.

"That she does," Click agreed, realizing his mistake as soon as Woodrow's smile vanished.

Luckily, Pearl was gone or the old man would have scared her into hiding. He, on the other hand, stood his ground.

"I'm doing my best to be cordial, boy, seeing as how you lost your kin." He straightened, lowering his voice. "I talked to my sister this morning. She told me you ran off and left Tandy in the hospital."

Click stared at the older man. "That's what she said?" he asked. He remembered it differently. Tandy had been inconsolable after they'd taken Amelia. And her mother... He swallowed. He hadn't run off, he'd been told to leave.

But Woodrow was right, he had left Tandy when she'd needed him.

"You saying my sister lied to me?" he asked.

Click swallowed down his anger. Susan Boone lived to stir the pot then stand back to see what sort of crisis she'd brought to the surface. He wasn't going to give her the satisfaction. He sucked in a deep breath, doing his best to stay calm. Woodrow Boone's opinion of him shouldn't matter. Only Tandy's. "I'd never leave her. Not by my choosing."

Woodrow's brows rose. "Seems to me you did, deserting her that way. Now leave the poor girl alone. You can't expect her to move on, with you showing up—bringing an angel along to help charm your way back in." He shook his head. "According to Susan, you didn't wait too long before you'd fathered your daughter. Now you're on your own, needing a hand and a mother for that sweet little thing. She's not going to turn her back on you, not after what she's lost. Tandy's too bighearted to see that you're using her, but I'm not. Might as well tell me what you're selling Lynnie's place for—I'll take it off your hands and you can be on your way."

Click saw red. He'd never use Tandy that way. Never willingly hurt her again. Tandy *was* bighearted, lonely and vulnerable. He wanted to believe she *wanted* to be where she was, with him and Pearl. That she wanted them. But the older man's words kicked up a flare of doubt.

"Uncle Woodrow?" Tandy had returned, holding Pearl's hand in one hand and a guitar in the other. He didn't know how long she'd been standing there or what she'd heard, but it was enough. "What's going on?"

Pearl hid behind Tandy, the tension in the room mounting until it was palpable. He didn't like the fear in his daughter's eyes.

"Woodrow?" Evelyn Boone joined her husband, her concern sincere. "We were having such a lovely evening."

Click knew the right thing to do. "It was. And I thank you kindly for your hospitality. But it's time for Pearl and I to head home." He wasn't going to cause a scene. He'd leave before things escalated. Tandy hadn't shared what had happened between them for a reason. He was pretty sure she'd be horrified for it to come out this way.

"Click?" Tandy's voice was soft.

He smiled. "I should go."

"No." Tandy stiffened, her eyes searching his before she faced her uncle. "Click is a good man, Uncle Woodrow. He always has been. I don't want to know what my mother's said to you, but I can tell you the truth. If I thought it would change how you felt about him. Or how you treat him."

Woodrow huffed, scowling at his niece. "A good man doesn't leave a woman in a hospital bed."

Click scooped up Pearl. "This is a conversation for behind closed doors, Mr. Boone." He glanced around the room. It was Sunday, so there was no organized activity for the guests. But the Boones ate all their meals in the guest dining room. And right now, gathered around the fireplace in the main living room, there were a handful of guests within earshot.

"What's happening?" Evelyn Boone asked.

"Mom." Scarlett's voice was soft as she hooked her arm through her mother's. "Dad. Click is right. Family business shouldn't be aired in public."

Woodrow's face turned a dark shade of red, but he didn't move.

"I won't presume to speak for Tandy." He lowered his

voice, moving closer. "But I'm asking you, as an honor-
able man, to keep what you've learned to yourself. It's
not about me—no one in Fort Kyle has ever given a damn
about me. The only reason that's changed now is because
Lynnie left me her place." He paused, watching the play
of emotions on the older man's face. "But Tandy…" He
glanced at her. "The more you talk, the more you'll hurt
her. I won't stand by and let that happen."

Woodrow Boone's gaze swept over him, head to toe.
But he didn't say a word.

"Da da, go?" Pearl whispered, her little voice shaking. "Ta-dee?"

"Yep, time to go." He smiled at his daughter, hugging her. "Ready, snuggle bunny?" He nodded at Evelyn, winked at Scarlett and smiled at Tandy before
carrying Pearl from the room. He kept moving, calm
and collected, until Pearl was buckled into her car seat.
He moved around the truck and climbed into the driver's
seat, wishing he could rewind the last five minutes. The
mix of anger and frustration, sadness and failure churn-
ing in his stomach had him shaking. Not that he could
blame Woodrow Boone for thinking ill of him. His sister
had probably made him sound like the lowest of the low.

There were times he wondered if the woman wasn't
right. He wasn't worthy of Tandy, wasn't capable of loving a person without hurting them.

"Da do go?" Pearl chattered from the back seat.

He stared at his daughter. But, if that was true, he had
no business fighting for custody of Pearl—if it came to
that. He couldn't imagine a future without his daughter in it.

"Waiting on me?" Tandy said, climbing into the passenger seat.

"Ta-dee?" Pearl called from the back seat.

"I'm here," Tandy said. "And I stole Uncle Woodrow's guitar." She laughed.

Click looked at her. "Probably not the best idea."

"You withdrawing your earlier offer? A place for Banshee and me to stay?" Her gaze was steady.

"Bashee," Pearl added. "Go, Da da."

Click sighed. "I don't want to cause problems between you and your family."

"*You* never have." She shook her head. "Now let's go home so we can feed Banshee and sing a couple of songs."

"You're sure?" he asked. "I don't need help."

"I know. This is where I want to be." She nodded.

He was breathing easier as he put the truck in gear and eased out of the parking lot.

"Mew-sik?" Pearl asked. "Sing, Ta-dee."

Tandy sang Lynnie's lullaby, about the pretty little horses, all the way home. He hummed along, wanting to ease some of the evening's hurt away. Pearl was still singing along when he carried her in the house.

"Ba-shee," Pearl greeted the dog, dropping a kiss on his head. "Yum-yum?" she asked.

Banshee stood, his tail wagging.

"So he speaks baby talk, too?" Click asked, watching the dog follow Pearl to the pantry, where his dog food had been stored.

"Like you said, he's smart." Tandy smiled up at him. She pressed one hand against his cheek, running the other through his thick hair. "You okay?"

"Now?" He smiled. *This is where I want to be.* She had no idea how she made him feel. He leaned forward to whisper, "Right now I'm pretty damn good."

Chapter Fifteen

Tandy sat on the edge of her bed, working a comb through the tangles and knots in her hair. She stared out the back window, the pitch of night dotted with a million sparkling stars and a sliver of bright white moon. On the horizon she could make out the razor-sharp edge of the distant cliffs and mountains. The seam where sky and land met seemed oddly fitting tonight, jagged and sudden. Her uncle's words had done the same—abruptly ending a lovely evening with angry, cutting words.

She'd seen the hurt in Click's eyes, felt the wound as if it were her own.

Banshee pushed her knee with his nose and whimpered.

"What?" she asked. "You don't want to sleep with me?"

He looked at her, groaning softly.

She smiled. "I know, fine." Banshee stopped sleeping on the bed around six months old. He was too big. Now he preferred a nice patch of floor, preferably near a window, where he could stretch out and snore. And boy did he snore. "Go on," she said, opening her bedroom door and watching him trot down the hallway—at the same time Click rounded the corner, carrying a glass of water.

"Hi," she said, her heart picking up. Every inch of her responded to the heat in his eyes.

"Hi." He stopped, his gaze wandering over her camisole and panties. His jaw clenched tightly, his fingers tightening around the glass he held.

She smiled. "Coming to bed?"

One dark eyebrow arched. "Inviting me in?"

"It was a standing invitation," she said.

The corner of his mouth kicked up. "I forgot the baby monitor," he said, heading back into the kitchen.

She slid into bed, anticipation igniting in her stomach and spreading like wildfire. Just thinking about their earlier kiss, the touch of his hands and fingers on her skin, had her aching.

By the time he'd plugged in Pearl's monitor and turned to look at her, it took all of her self-control not to attack him. Something that got ten times harder when he tugged his skintight white T-shirt over his head and unbuttoned his jeans. He was gorgeous.

She tore her gaze from the rock-hard expanse of his chest and abdomen, worrying the quilt between her fingers.

"I saw your message from Miss Francis," he said, sitting on the side of the bed. "You up for a trip to Alpine tomorrow?"

She nodded, too breathless to sound coherent.

He flipped off the overhead light and lay back on the pillow, his hand taking hers. "Tired?" he asked, his voice deep and gruff.

She shook her head. Sleep was the last thing on her mind.

"Tandy?"

She sat up, turned on the bedside lamp and stared at him. "I'm not tired." Her voice shook.

His blue eyes blazed into hers.

She hesitated, overwhelmed with need. It helped that he felt the same. That his hands gripped the quilt and his chest rose and fell too quickly. She closed the distance between them as she climbed on top of him, straddling him. His eyes widened, the muscle in his jaw clenched, as she leaned forward to press her curves against the angles of his chest.

He was warm beneath her hands. Her fingers ran along the sides of his neck to trace his jawline. His eyes bore into hers as she cradled his cheek and brushed her lips against his.

He moaned against her lips as he touched her. Finally. His hands slid up her sides, finding their way beneath her thin camisole. She arched into him, her lips parting his as his hands pressed against her back.

Her fingers threaded through his thick hair, giving her something to hold on to—to anchor herself as when his kiss made the world fall away. The stroke of his tongue was intoxicating. When his mouth descended to her neck, pressing light, wet kisses to her sensitive skin, she shuddered. His lips sucked her earlobe into his mouth, nipping gently before moving down, around her neck and to her collarbone.

She held on, yearning for more. His hands drifted to her hips, giving her the room to slide her camisole up and off.

"You're beautiful," he whispered, staring up at her. He ran his fingers along the cleft between her breasts, sweeping his fingers under the swell and teasing her senses. She arched forward, crying out when his mouth latched on to her nipple.

She ended up under him, the quilts tossed aside as he kissed her deeply. His hand clasped her breast, his finger and thumb stroking her to a feverish point. She moaned, her nails scouring his shoulders when his mouth left her to nuzzle and suck her inflamed nipple. First one, then the other, he seemed intent on making her body come alive. Before she came apart.

She couldn't stop touching him. So many things had changed, but not her fascination with his body. The strength of his arms. The line of his back. The quiver of his stomach when her hands dipped beneath the elastic of his boxer shorts. He was all muscle. And all hers.

Her eyes fluttered open then, reeling by the look on his face. He was lost in exploration, watching his hands on her body. Every gasp she made, every shudder or tremble, pleasing him. She pressed a hand to his cheek, loving the kiss he pressed against her palm. Her hand slid up, tangling in his hair, to pull him down to her.

When his gaze met hers, he smiled.

And that smile knocked the last of her walls down. It was still there, stronger than ever. She loved him. Whatever their past was, their love had endured. She knew that now. This was right. He was home—that hadn't changed.

His kiss was soft, his lips moving over hers until she was gasping for breath. When her lips parted, his tongue slipped inside.

Her hands tugged at his boxers, sliding them down his hip. She wanted him, needed him—no more waiting. He was gone long enough to remove his boxers, long enough for her to wriggle out of her panties. He lifted her foot, sliding the fabric free.

Her eyes drifted shut when he kissed her ankle, her knee, her hip and side. Sensation took over. His rough fingertips stroked gently over one breast, then the other, before the wet heat of his mouth worshipped them. She gripped his shoulders, pulling him up, craving what was next. His hands cradled her face as he kissed her. She gazed up at him, panting and flushed and desperate.

"Click," she whispered. "Love me, please."

HER BODY OFFERED pure pleasure. Every curve begged for his attention. He couldn't get enough of the taste of her skin. The broken whimper she made when he touched her made him throb and ache. The bite of her nails on his back spurred him on. Her scent wrapped around him, until he drew her into his lungs. He was drowning in her, focused on her and only her, and loving every minute of it.

She was so damn beautiful. So close to falling apart.

He ran his fingers down her side, stroking her hip and thigh. Her legs parted, pulling a groan from his chest. She wanted him. He couldn't wait any longer.

His lips found hers as he moved between her legs. Her hands gripped his shoulders, her breath hitching as he clasped her hips. He thrust into her, slowly, watching her face as he sank deep inside her. She arched back into the pillow, the broken gasp spilling from her lips almost shaking his resolve to make this last. He closed his eyes, digging deep for control.

How many times had he dreamed of this? Of loving her? Now that he was, he'd make sure she knew how special this was to him. How special she was. It was Tandy's hand pressed against his cheek. Her soft lips pressed against his, seeking his kiss. He stared down at her, smiling at the tenderness on her face. He loved this woman, mind, body and soul.

She was flushed and beautiful beneath him. When he thrust, she moaned, her fingers pressing into his back. Her gaze met his, stunned and reeling and so hungry for him Click forgot about control. His rhythm picked up, over and over, the brush of her skin and shudder of her breath driving him on. It was sweet torture, friction and heat, as they came together again and again.

He kissed her, latching on to her lower lip and drawing another quiver from her body. "I missed you, Tandy."

She stiffened beneath him, arching up against him as her muscles contracted. He watched, mesmerized, as her release found her. Her hands gripped him tightly against her as she cried out against his lips. Her eyes fluttered open as her body convulsed around him—and pushed him over the edge. He held her hips, driving into her until his body shook with his climax. It crashed into him, knocking the breath from his lungs and spiraling him into sensation.

He rolled off her, gasping and boneless as he pulled her into his arms. She burrowed close against his side, resting her head on his chest. There was no way she could miss the thundering of his heart. Not that he could do a damn thing about it—it was how she affected him. It took time for his breathing to slow, but his hold on her didn't ease. She was back in his arms, and he was in no hurry to let her go.

She looked up at him, slowly stroking his chest.

He ran his fingers over the curve of her cheek and smiled.

"You should smile more often," she said.

"I'll work on it," he offered.

She nodded. "Do that."

He arched a brow. "Anything else I need to work on?"

She shook her head.

"Nothing?" His thumb traced her jaw.

"I wouldn't change a thing." Her hazel-green gaze met his.

"A man could get lost in those eyes," he whispered, stroking her brow. "I know I did. For hours at a time."

She grinned. "Are you complaining?"

"No, ma'am." He ran his fingers through her hair and smiled.

"There it is," she said, pressing her fingers to his lips.

He caught her hand, kissing her fingertips, her palm and the inside of her wrist. She leaned up, brushing a featherlight kiss on his mouth.

"Tired now?" he asked.

She shook her head. "You?"

He kissed her, his lips clinging just long enough to make her breath hitch. "No."

She rested her chin on his chest, her eyes traveling slowly over his face. He didn't mind. Looking at her made this real. He kept thinking he was going to wake up, alone and frantic, in his bed.

"I saw your note," Tandy said, interrupting his thoughts.

"Note?" he repeated, smoothing her hair back.

"Pearl. And Georgia." She watched him closely. "I don't want to pry."

He shook his head. "I know."

"Can I ask when she'll be here?"

"You can ask me anything," he whispered, holding her chin until she looked at him. "Okay?"

She nodded. "How much longer does she have in the rehabilitation facility?"

"A couple more weeks to go. She thinks she'll be done at the sixty-day mark." He sighed. "She's planning on heading straight here."

Tandy frowned. "She is?"

He nodded. He didn't like it either. He was just figuring his baby girl out. Now he was supposed to hand her over? Georgia hadn't said much beyond her expected release date and a few questions about Pearl. Namely, if she was okay. Click had done his best to assure her they were getting along.

"But… She can't just take her, can she?" she asked.

He shook his head. "I'm going to talk to Kevin Glenn tomorrow, see what my options are. I know I haven't had her long, but… I'm having a hell of a hard time imagining her not being here."

She nodded, a deep furrow settling in between her brows. "And Georgia. Is she…is she a good person? I mean, I don't mean to sound uncharitable, but is she what's best for Pearl?"

Tandy was saying what he'd been thinking. "I can't say. I knew her from the circuit." He glanced at her. "She wasn't interested in settling down."

"So you knew her well?" she asked, her tone tight.

Shame pressed in on him. "No. I didn't. But I saw her in action."

Tandy was staring at his chest.

He knew what she was thinking. "I left you and headed to Lynnie's. I stopped at a bar on the circuit, and she was there. I don't remember much else, Tandy. I can't change what happened. I'm sure as hell not proud of it—"

"Some good came from it." Her eyes shone with unshed tears. "You got Pearl."

He nodded, his arms tightening around her. "I did." He cleared his throat. "Now I have to find a way to keep her."

Chapter Sixteen

Tandy and Pearl made blueberry muffins for breakfast. Pearl had bright blue fingertips by the time they were done and the kitchen was a mess, but Click's laughter made it all worth it. When they were done with the pile of dishes, they dressed to go into town.

Click dropped her off for her doctor's checkup and drove out to pick Miss Francis up. By the time he was back, Tandy was done.

"A clean bill of health," she said, sliding into the back seat by Pearl's car seat.

"That's wonderful news, Tandy," Miss Francis said. "Click was telling me all about it. Stitches and a flattened house?" She tsk-tsked before going on. "Sounds like having your neighbor around sure came in handy."

"Thank God for her dog," Click said.

Tandy smiled at Click in the rearview mirror, loving the way the corners of his eyes crinkled when he smiled.

"Keep your eyes on the road, son," Miss Francis said, patting Click's hand on the steering wheel.

Tandy laughed. The road was wide open and empty as far as the eye could see, but she wasn't going to say a word to challenge Miss Francis.

"Ta-dee?" Pearl said, leaning forward in her seat.

"Hi, Pearl." She rummaged through the box on the floorboard. "How about we read a book?"

Pearl nodded, so Tandy read her a book all about penguins. Pearl was sound asleep before she reached the halfway mark.

"Well, what happens next?" Miss Francis asked.

"I think Pearl dozed off," Click said, chuckling.

"I'll read the rest of it on the way back," Tandy offered.

Miss Francis laughed. "You two are doing a fine job with her." She paused. "I never doubted it once, mind you. Now that you're staying put, seems like you should make it all proper. A big wedding, with all the fixings. You don't want people talking."

Miss Francis's words were like a cold shower. Words like *you two* and *big wedding* and *staying put* implied things. Things she and Click hadn't talked about. Things that could hurt her all over again.

Pearl wasn't her daughter. She was Click's. And Georgia's.

Tandy stared out the window, her pulse kicking up.

"You young people wait too long to settle down and start a family. You want to be young enough to run after your grandkids, take it from me. Nothing worse than a grandma that's stuck in a rocking chair." Miss Francis shook her head. "You could have it at the old fort. Makes for pretty pictures. Or the observatory—at night. My, that would be quite the thing."

"We'd have to talk to our wedding planners," Click said. "They've already got it all worked out."

"Wedding planners?" Miss Francis asked.

"He's teasing you, Miss Francis," Tandy spoke up. "Click's being kind enough to let me use a spare room, that's all." She could feel Click's gaze on her in the rearview mirror but couldn't look at him.

"Click Hale." Miss Francis sighed. "You shouldn't tease a woman my age about things like that. I was about to get the quilting group started on a wedding-ring quilt for you. And talk to Mabelle about putting aside some bulbs for flowers. And to the Buchanan family about the printers they used for their daughters' weddings. Such nice invitations."

Tandy shook her head and frowned at Click. This was how stories got started. Stories that people in a small town would spread like wildfire. And when things fell apart, all those people would be looking for the reasons they fell apart, making it that much worse—that much harder to get away from.

She pressed her eyes closed.

"I'm sorry, Miss Francis." Click chuckled. "You'll be the first one to know when Tandy and I decide to make things proper."

"See that you do," Miss Francis said. "Now, I have my list…"

Tandy listened to the old woman list off the stops they'd need to make before they could head back to Fort Kyle.

"I figure Tandy will want to stop there, pick up some clothing. Might find a few things for Pearl, too, since she's likely growing like a weed." Miss Francis kept on going.

Tandy smiled at Pearl, sound asleep in her car seat, and took Pearl's little hand in hers. She had no claim on this child, but Tandy loved her all the same. Would she get the chance to see Pearl grow up, run on sturdy legs, speak in full sentences and sing like a songbird?

Click was worried. He tried to act calm, but she'd

seen the fear in his eyes. He was worried about losing his daughter.

There wasn't a thing she could do to help him.

It wasn't fair.

He'd already lost one daughter, he shouldn't lose Pearl, too.

She rested her head against the car seat and studied Click's profile as he talked with Miss Francis. They were discussing the costs of Click irrigating part of his land for crops. And, if he did irrigate, what he'd grow. With the frequent drought-like conditions in this part of Texas, investing in crops was a risk. If he did irrigate and plant crops, the local wildlife would find his spread too good to refuse. Whatever he decided, he'd make it work. That was the way Click was, determined—committed.

She didn't know much about Pearl's mother. She wasn't sure she wanted to. What she did know didn't recommend the woman for motherhood. It wasn't the sleeping around that gave Tandy pause. Her brother had visited more than his fair share of beds when he was foot-loose and fancy-free. Drug use was different.

Pearl rubbed her eyes, her head shifting to the other side of the car seat. She slept on, oblivious to the conversation in the front seat or Tandy holding her hand.

This baby girl's future was unknown. As much as Tandy loved her, she had no say-so in her future. Just like before—with Amelia. When she'd been helpless to do anything as her baby was taken from her. Pain sliced sharply through her chest, so sharp she pressed her hand to her chest. She wasn't strong enough to go through that again. Maybe she should stop the pain before it destroyed her. But was she strong enough to leave Click and Pearl? Giving up her chance at happiness was the only way to protect herself from irreparable heartbreak.

"You're in a mighty fine position," Kevin Glenn said. "Property, income, character references. The things the court wants in a custody case."

"I don't know if it's going to come to that." Click tapped his fingers on the tabletop.

"Best to be prepared," Mr. Glenn said. "What do we know about Georgia Miles?"

"Not much," Click confessed.

"Well, what we do know won't hurt us." Mr. Glenn sat back, taking a sip of the sweet tea Tandy had made earlier. "Thought about hiring a private investigator? I know you don't want to play hardball, son, and I respect that. But I'm thinking your daughter's needs should come first. You say she's in a drug rehabilitation facility? Was this her choice or court required?"

"Her choice, I think." Click ran a hand over his face. He didn't want to be in this position.

"Wouldn't hurt to find out," Kevin Glenn said. "Just in case."

"Like I said, I'm hoping it won't come to that." He stopped tapping his fingers on the table and pressed his hands against his thighs. "This whole business makes me uncomfortable, Mr. Glenn."

"I understand, Click, I do." He nodded. "If she shows up wanting to take Pearl, we'll file an injunction. That way there's a formal custody arrangement worked out and you won't worry you'll never see your daughter again."

That he could agree to. He wasn't going to lose his daughter.

"But if she shows up with some fancy lawyer, I want you to consider hiring a private eye. Now that you've got all this, she might get greedy and go after more than just custody." Mr. Glenn slid his tablet into his beaten-up briefcase and stood. "You have any questions, you call me."

"I appreciate you coming out so late." Click walked the older man to the front door.

"The wife had bingo at the community center, so it worked out fine." He grinned. "Couldn't help but notice the improvements you've made on the place when I got here. Things are looking good, Click. New fences, fresh coat of paint on the barn, and graveled the driveway, too. Been busy. I hear tell you're thinking about starting a training facility? For cutting horses? Your specialty?" The older man cast an appreciative gaze over Click's land.

"Word sure travels fast."

"No secrets in a town this size." He chuckled. "Like Tandy Boone staying here?"

"We weren't trying to keep that a secret. She was staying there." He pointed at the cabin. "It's not like I don't have the room. She's a real help with Pearl, too." Which was true. After their run-in, Woodrow Boone couldn't be happy about his niece moving in, but he hadn't sent anyone or anything to clear the wreckage away. So Click had repaired that part of the fence first, reinforcing the sheep and goat wiring and putting in new fence stays to make sure the goats, Banshee and Pearl didn't wander that way.

"She can't stay there. No, sirree," Mr. Glenn agreed. "That'd be downright dangerous. How long she staying with you?"

Click glanced at the older man. "I didn't give her a deadline."

Mr. Glenn scratched his chin. "I was real fond of your aunt, Click. And she was real fond of you. So I'm just going to come right out with it. I'm not telling you what to do here, but it might be best for Miss Boone to find someplace else to rest her pretty little head. Just until this custody business is done and over."

Click met the old man's gaze. There was no judgment there, just concern. "I appreciate that," he said.

Mr. Glenn smiled and made his way to his truck. "Like your new ride, Click." He touched the rim of his beaten cowboy hat before driving away.

Click leaned against the porch railing, savoring the silence. The sky was a deep blue, darker each second. The wind was constant, but it didn't howl like the day of the storm. It whispered, carrying with it the sounds of the plains. Rustling grass, the distant bleat of the goat and snort of his horses, the call of a black hawk hunting mice. It was peaceful.

"Click?" Tandy joined him on the porch. "She was sound asleep before I covered her with her blanket."

He slid an arm around her. "It's been a long day."

She studied him, staying stiff in his hold. "Did Mr. Glenn have good news?"

"I'm not sure I'd call it good news." He pressed a kiss to her forehead. "If it comes to a court case, there's a chance it could get personal."

"What does that mean?" she asked.

"Digging into her past. Digging into mine. Weighing who's better for Pearl." He sighed. "I don't want to lose Pearl, but I don't want to deprive her of her mother. If Georgia's turned her life around, Pearl deserves to have her in her life." But his heart hurt at the thought of not seeing her every day. He hadn't planned on being a father. Now that he was, he didn't want to be part-time. His arms tightened around Tandy, needing her comfort. But she stayed rigid, almost braced. He frowned down at her. "What's wrong?"

"I heard what he said. About me staying here." Her voice dropped. "I think he's right."

"I don't," he argued.

She pushed out of his hold. "I do."

He tried to stay calm, gripping the porch railing for support. "Tandy, I need you here—"

"No, you don't." She shook her head. "You need to do what's right for Pearl. And you. And I need to do what's right for me."

Warning bells went off in his head. She wouldn't look at him, wouldn't touch him… "Talk to me."

"I just did." She wrapped her arms around her waist "I… I'm not going to complicate things with Pearl and her…mother." She blew out a slow breath. "We've both been through too much. You're stronger than me. You have a reason to keep fighting." She glanced his way. It was quick, but it was enough. The pain and fear in her eyes gripped him by the throat.

"*We* can do this," he rasped. Two months ago he was alone. The possibility of a family, a home or making plans for the future never entered his mind. Now he had Pearl and Tandy and this place.

"I don't think I can," she admitted. "I need space."

Headlights appeared.

"That's Scarlett," Tandy said.

Click's heart thudded heavily in his chest. All he could do was stand there, watching, while she loaded her suitcase into Scarlett's truck. If she said something else, he didn't hear it. She'd said he had a reason to keep fighting. He'd hoped she had one, too. He'd hoped she'd fight for him, for them. And it tore his heart out to know he was wrong.

Chapter Seventeen

The next week had her falling into a sort of routine. As long as Tandy didn't give herself time to think, she managed.

After breakfast at Fire Gorge, she drove one of the old ranch trucks into Fort Kyle—to Dr. Edwards's clinic. Some days she worked at the clinic, other days she was in the mobile unit. Dr. Edwards was still disorganized and distracted, but Tandy didn't let it get to her. Her new philosophy was all about wearing herself out, no matter how many extra hours she put in or how many patients she saw.

No matter how hard she worked, every night was the same. Her heart ached for Click and Pearl. She'd pick up the phone to call him, to hear his voice and know he was okay. Every day she doubted what she'd done.

"You got a letter today," Scarlett said, handing her the gold-embossed envelope.

University of East Texas College of Veterinary Medicine. "Guess they weren't sure I got the first rejection letter," she said. "I'm going to shower."

"You're not going to read it?" Scarlett asked.

She closed the bathroom door, shrugging out of her clothes as she called out, "Go ahead." She stood under the hot water, washing away the dust and animal hair.

Her stomach growled loudly. There'd been so much to do she'd forgotten to eat, again.

Scarlett's pounding had her turning off the water before she was ready.

"I'm coming," she said, wrapping a towel around herself and stepping out. "Give me sec."

"Open the door, Tandy," Scarlett said.

Tandy yanked the door open. "What's wrong?"

"Nothing." She held the letter up to Tandy's face. "Nothing at all. Read it."

We are pleased to inform you that a space has become available for the next academic year. In order to accept the spot, please reply by... Tandy snatched the paper from Scarlett's fingers and read it again.

"You're getting it all wet," Scarlett argued.

"I was in the shower," she murmured, stunned. She was in—finally. Which was good. Great. Wasn't it?

"Good news, right?" Scarlett asked.

Poor Scarlett had picked her up from Click's without asking a single question. Every day, she chattered away as if she understood Tandy couldn't bear to talk about whatever had happened. And for that, Tandy was thankful.

"Yes." Tandy hugged her, not sure what to think or feel. "It's great news." So why wasn't she more excited? And why did she want to share the good news with Click?

"We should do something to celebrate," Scarlett said, smiling widely. "But, Dad needs me. I'll be back later. We'll go do something?"

Tandy nodded. "Of course. Yes. Go on." She waved her toward the door and sat on the edge of the bed, staring at her letter.

She read the letter again and again, searching for the excitement she'd imagined.

The strumming of a guitar had her digging through her things for her cell phone.

Click.

She stared at it, the guitar ringtone strumming again and again.

"Hello?" she answered.

Pearl's cries echoed through the receiver.

"What's wrong?" she asked, standing.

"Pearl's got an ear infection. She's had her meds but… she wants you." His voice was gruff. "I didn't want to bother you, but she won't calm down."

Bother her? She didn't need to think about her answer. Pearl was sick and wanted her. "I'll be there soon." She hung up and started shrugging into clean clothes.

In less than five minutes she was headed to Click's—tangled mop of wet hair and all. Pearl would eventually stop crying, logically she knew this. And that she was putting herself right back in the vulnerable position that scared her. But it didn't matter. She kept driving. Apparently, all it took to set aside her sense of self-preservation was Pearl's cries.

Banshee bailed out of the truck as soon as they arrived, Pearl's wails spilling out into the country air. Tandy followed quickly, pushing through the front door without knocking. She didn't look at Click, not yet—she was here for Pearl.

"Ta-dee," Pearl hiccuped, reaching for her as soon as she saw her. "Bashee."

Tandy took one look at Pearl's tear-streaked red face and knew she'd done the right thing. "Poor baby," she whispered, hugging the toddler close. "I'm sorry you feel bad, snuggle bunny." She patted her back.

"Doc said it was pretty bad." Click's voice was low. "She's real congested, too."

She could tell. Beneath her hand, Pearl's lungs wheezed. Poor Pearl. And poor Click. Having a sick baby was scary—especially the first time. She glanced at him, noting the tension in his shoulders and the shadows beneath his eyes. "I know it hurts, snuggle bunny, but you're going to be okay." She sat in the rocking chair and started humming.

Pearl shuddered and hiccuped against her, one little hand reaching up to twine in her loose hair. Slowly Pearl calmed, her little voice mirroring Tandy's.

It was the sweetest sound.

Tandy drew in a deep breath and risked another look Click's way. She wasn't prepared for the anger that blazed there. He'd called her but he wasn't happy about it.

Why would he be? She'd deserted them. Him… Again. When he needed her most. Because she'd let her fear take over—and made the biggest mistake of her life.

Pearl coughed, the heavy barking sound making Click wince.

"Did the doctor talk about getting a nebulizer?" she asked.

He nodded. "Set up in the bedroom already. Gave her a bath in some vapor stuff that stinks to the high heavens, too."

She smiled at him. He had no idea how amazing he was. "You've done all the right things."

He ran a hand over his face, clearly agitated. "She's sick. That's on me."

"Kids get sick, Click." She kept patting Pearl's back, kept her voice calm. "It's not your fault."

His eyes slammed into her. "I don't like it."

The raw frustration in his voice was so sincere Tandy stopped the smile his words stirred up. Pearl wasn't the only one who needed comfort. Click looked like his last nerve was stretched taut. Her defection probably hadn't helped. She kept rocking and humming, trying to think of a way to break the thickening silence. How could she undo what she'd done? But words wouldn't come.

"She asleep?" Click asked, his voice low and soothing—for Pearl.

Tandy peered down at Pearl, her warm cheek pressed against her chest and her breathing even and deep. "I think so."

"I can put her down." His words were hard. "You can go."

He spoke without malice—but it hurt all the same. "I can do it. I don't want to wake her." She didn't want to go. She didn't want to move. As sorry as she was that Pearl was sick, she'd ached for the sweet weight of this little girl in her arms. She wasn't in a rush to give her up or leave him.

He nodded, stiff. "Okay." The word hitched, forcing her to look at him.

The sorrow and yearning on his face mirrored her own. Her heart shuddered, reminding her how irrevocably she was tied to him. Risky or no, there was no way she could walk away from this man. Not really. She had to find the courage and strength to fix this. "Click. I need to talk to you."

He cleared his throat, the muscle in his jaw working. He opened his mouth, then clamped it shut. "Okay."

Headlights bounced off the far wall, momentarily blinding them.

His gaze traveled over her face before he nodded. "Give me a second. Not expecting anyone. Unless Delgado sent some more men out," he murmured, pushing through the front door. He caught it at the last minute, before it could bounce of the wall and disturb Pearl.

Because that's the way Click was—thoughtful and caring.

She pressed a kiss to Pearl's temple. "I'm an idiot, Pearl. An idiot." Tears stung her eyes. How had she let the fear of what might happen steal her happiness? Life wasn't always easy or fair, but she had Click. She had love. Real love.

She stood, causing Pearl to jolt awake.

"Sorry, snuggle bunny," she whispered.

Pearl rested her head and patted Tandy's chest. "Da da?"

"Let's go find him. You can give him night-night kisses. Okay?"

Pearl nodded.

But finding Click talking to a fair-haired woman was unexpected. Click's posture was telling, but the flash of panic on his face when he saw her— saw Pearl—told Tandy exactly what she needed to know. Click wasn't talking to a potential employee.

This had to be Georgia Miles. Pearl's mother.

"I SHOULD HAVE left a message," Georgia said again. "I didn't know what to say. You know?"

He knew exactly what she meant. This whole situation left him speechless. He was scared—not wanting to lose his daughter or make a mistake with the woman who might try to take her from him. Click shrugged. "You're here now."

Pearl and Banshee walked along the fence line, without a care in the world. His daughter was too young to remember much. She'd hugged Georgia then toddled after Banshee—determined not to let her favorite four-legged pal out of her sight.

"I don't think she remembers me," Georgia said.

"She's walking so well. She started early, though. At nine months she was ready to go."

Pearl stooped to pick up a stray chicken feather and held it out to Banshee. The dog sniffed it, then sneezed. Pearl's laughter was a stark contrast to her earlier tantrum.

Click smiled at his daughter. "She's always on the move, that's for sure."

Pearl let Banshee kiss her cheek.

"That dog is awful big," Georgia said.

"And smart," Click said. "He takes good care of her."

"So, you two are doing well?"

He glanced at her, bracing himself. "Yes." If she could ask, so could he. "How are you doing?" She looked different from what he remembered. Not that he remembered her all that well. The few times they'd met, she'd been hanging off someone's arm, smiling—and drunk. Now, she looked older, wary. And bone-tired.

Her light brown eyes—the same color as Pearl's eyes—met his. "It's been hard. It is hard."

He nodded. Part of him wanted to rip off the Band-Aid and see what she wanted. The other part wanted to keep dancing around the subject to avoid answers he might not like. Tandy didn't want him in her life anymore. He couldn't lose Pearl, too.

"I didn't mean to chase off your friend," Georgia said, glancing back at the house. "Pearl seems to like her."

He nodded again. Pearl adored Tandy. And Tandy loved his little girl. He blew out a deep breath, trying to ease the tension there. "She's giving us privacy."

Georgia sighed. "I'm at the hotel in town for a couple of nights, so we can sort things out."

"Things?" Click asked, an undeniable edge to his voice.

She sighed again. "Pearl."

Pearl turned around and toddled back to them. "Hi."

Georgia smiled at her, dropping to her knees. "Hi to you, too."

Pearl's gaze traveled from Georgia to Click. She smiled then toddled back to Banshee, patted the dog and kept on walking. Georgia stayed where she was, watching her daughter with smudged eyes. "She seems happy." Her voice was soft.

"I've been trying my hardest, Georgia. She's pretty easy to please." He watched Pearl stoop to pick up something in the dirt.

"You've done a good job," she said. "Thank you."

He didn't want her thanks. He wanted to keep his daughter. He swallowed, nodding.

"I should probably go," she said. "I don't know my way around, and it's getting late."

"Come out for lunch tomorrow?" he asked.

"Sure," she said. "Sounds like a plan." She stopped. "Guess I'll head back. Bye bye, Pearl."

Pearl looked back, her little chin quivering. She shook her head, those black curls bouncing. She ran to him, her little hands reaching for him. "Dada…"

He knelt, holding her tightly to his chest. "I got you, Pearl. No bye-bye."

She nodded, burying her face against his shirt.

"I'll see you tomorrow." Georgia's voice wobbled.

She was hurting. What the hell was he supposed to do? He felt for the woman, he did. But his loyalties lay with his daughter. "We'll walk you back," he said, scooping Pearl up. "Come on, Banshee."

"You miss the circuit?" she asked as they walked. "Your life before midnight feedings and dirty diapers?"

He didn't have to think about his answer. "No."

"Wish they made more men like you, Click." She shook her head. "You almost restore a gal's hope in the opposite sex."

It took all of his self-control to point out that bars might not be the best place for relationship material. But it wasn't his place. She was trying to get her life together. That was a good place to start. They walked on, the house growing larger. Tandy had turned on the kitchen and parlor lights, making the windows glow with invitation. And she was inside—waiting to talk to him.

Home. This was home. He ran a hand over Pearl's back.

"So you're happy?" She paused, looking at him. "You look good. Damn good."

"I'm happy." He smiled at her.

She nodded, patting Pearl's back. "I'll see you tomorrow. Lunch." She climbed into her little car and drove down the driveway.

Click stood there until there was no sign of her taillights or dust kicked up on her exit. She was gone. He could finally breathe. His heart slowed, but the dull ache was there. Nothing was resolved, not yet.

Pearl yawned, reminding him it was past her bedtime. "Nighttime, snuggle bunny," he said, loving the way she curled into him. "I'm sorry you're feeling bad," he said, kissing Pearl's head.

Pearl shook her head. "Tadee sing."

Click nodded. "Maybe. Let's ask. Remember to say please." She'd stay, for Pearl. But he wanted her to stay for him—for them. He hoped like hell that was why she wanted to talk to him.

Pearl nodded, grinning. "Peez."

Tandy was in the kitchen, elbows deep in dishwater. A quick glance around the kitchen told him she hadn't been watching out the window. No, she'd been scrubbing down the kitchen. "Did she leave?" she asked, nervously looking between them.

He nodded. "For now." His words were thick.

"Sing peez?" Pearl asked, reaching for her. "Tadee?"

Tandy nodded, her eyes searching his. "Yes, ma'am." She wiped her hands on her apron and took Pearl's hand.

She was close—close enough to touch. Her scent rolled over him. It was hard not to reach for her, hard not to pull her close. "Kitchen looks nice. I appreciate it. And you coming out here. I know it's not…what you wanted."

Her brow furrowed. "Click…that's not true."

"Tadee, mew-sik," Pearl said, tugging her earlobe.

He stared at her long and hard, noting the flush of her cheeks. Hope washed over him—so much hope. "We're going to talk," he said to her. "But I need to make a quick call first. So there's nothing hanging over my head." He needed Kevin Glenn's counsel. It might make things easier if the man joined them for lunch tomorrow. He headed onto the back porch to make the call.

"How can I help you this evening?" Mr. Glenn asked.

"Georgia's here. She'll be coming out tomorrow for lunch to talk. I figured I'd touch base with you before that happened."

There was a pause. "Is she alone?"

"She was tonight." His gaze wandered along the fence line. Domino was at the water trough. Blackjack was dozing several feet away.

"You say she's coming for lunch?" Mr. Glenn said. "Maybe I'll stop by?"

"Sounds good. See you tomorrow," he said, hanging up.

Tandy played the piano, with Pearl's help from the sound of it. It brought a smile to his lips.

He patted Banshee's head, eager to hear what Tandy wanted to say—and terrified. "I'm hoping it's good news," he said to the dog. If he had Tandy at his side, he could handle whatever life threw at him.

Chapter Eighteen

Tandy rocked Pearl, rubbing a cool cloth across her fevered forehead. Poor Pearl was fighting sleep, her little fingers tugging on her right earlobe before she dissolved into a puddle of tears. After another vapor bath and a long lullaby-filled cuddle, Pearl had dozed off. But as soon as Tandy had laid her in her crib, Pearl had started to cry.

"I thought she'd be doing better." Click was pacing. He'd been pacing since she started crying again. "What's the point of making her take medicine if it's not going to help?"

"Her fever is down," Tandy tried to reassure him. "It'll take some time."

He sighed, slumping into the recliner opposite her rocking chair, one long leg stretching out. His boot caught on the strap of her purse, dumping its contents all over the floor.

"I'm sorry." He crouched, only to have Banshee come nose-to-nose with him. "Come on, Banshee." But every time Click moved, Banshee moved with him—thinking it was a game.

Tandy giggled, muffling her mouth with her hand.

It wasn't long before Click was laughing, too, sitting on the floor, Banshee trying his hardest to fit into his lap.

"Maybe he's feeling left out?" Tandy asked.

Click smiled at her, rubbing behind Banshee's ear. "Guess so."

She loved his smile. She loved how kind and patient he was. She loved the way a simple look made her feel cherished.

He loved her.

He cleared his throat and turned his attention to the mess on his floor. Click did his best to work around Banshee, collecting lipstick, Band-Aids, sunglasses, hand sanitizer, her notebook, some pictures of her brother and his family. "Toben's son?" he said, picking up the photo. "Cute kid."

She nodded. Pearl stirred, fussing just enough that Tandy shifted her. She stood, bouncing the baby in her arms. "I'm going to try to put her to bed." It took a bit of rocking and some back rubbing, but Pearl finally relaxed into a deep sleep.

Tandy stared at the sleeping baby. "Time to go beg your daddy for forgiveness, Pearl. Wish me luck." She took a deep breath and headed into the living room.

Click stood, reading her acceptance letter. "Is this what you wanted to talk to me about?"

She shook her head.

"This is a big deal, Tandy. You're getting what you always dreamed of. Congratulations." He cleared his throat, reading over the letter again. "I hear Stonewall Crossing is a nice place. Not so dry. Or so flat. They get rain once in a while."

She nodded. "It is pretty country. But there's something about Fire Gorge that's truly beautiful."

"I've driven from one end of the country to the other. Nothing compared to this." He nodded. "You'll miss it."

She frowned. "Why would I miss it?"

"You can't pass this up." He shook his head, holding out the letter.

"I'm not going," she said.

"Yes, you are." He frowned.

"I realized something when I got that letter," she said, closing the distance between them. "This didn't matter if I didn't have you to share it with. Tell me it's not too late, Click." She placed her hand on his arm. "Tell me you'll give me another chance. I'm scared of what could happen with Pearl. But what really terrifies me is life without you. I'm so sorry. You're what I want—you're always what I've wanted most."

He dropped the papers and pulled her into his arms, his warm hand pressed against her cheek. "I'm glad to hear it." He pressed a kiss to her forehead. "But I'm not letting you give up on your dream for me. I love you." He shook his head, studying her. "Your uncle would jump on this place. Pearl and I will be happy anywhere. As long as you're there." He smiled. "You lead, we'll follow."

She stared at him, stunned. "You'd do that?"

He nodded. "Yes, ma'am."

"Because you love me?" she whispered.

"Because I love you. Because you make life better." He smiled. "Complete. You are all I want. And all I need."

"You and me and Pearl?" she asked.

"Yes, ma'am." His gaze swept over her face.

"I don't want to leave this place," she said. "This is home—"

"Tandy." He frowned.

She covered his mouth. "We don't need to go. They have a distance program. There's information with the letter. Sure, I'd have to go to Stonewall Crossing a few times a month and Doc Edwards would have to sign off on my hours at the clinic, but it could work." The more she talked, the more excited she became. "Pearl could get to know her cousins. And you could talk to my uncle Teddy about training some of his horses or the refuge horses—"

He kissed her until she was swaying on her feet. Then she just held on to him.

"You're sure about staying here?" he asked, his lips brushing hers—teasing and featherlight.

She broke away from their kiss. "I'm being greedy, Click Hale. I want it all. I want to go to school, but I want you more." Her fingers stroked his lips. "Is that okay with you?"

He nodded. "I wouldn't let you settle for anything less."

"I know." She wrapped her arms around his neck. "That's why I gave you my heart, and a puppy, all those years ago."

The love in his smile washed over her. "After I'm done kissing you, we'll call our wedding planners and make this official and proper."

Epilogue

Click listened to the sound of Tandy's voice over the baby monitor as he finished loading the dishwasher. He could always tell when Pearl was asleep—it was when her little voice fell silent. She was a songbird, just like Tandy. And he loved it.

Banshee yawned from his spot in the corner.

"Tired, too?" he asked the dog. "She's getting harder to keep up with, isn't she?"

It was true. The bigger Pearl got, the faster she went. He didn't know what he'd do without Banshee tracking after her. The dog was like a canine nanny, keeping her corralled close to the house and alerting them to any signs of danger.

"Are you talking about me? I know I am," Tandy said as she crossed the room. She slid her arms around his waist and pressed her cheek against his back.

"Guess it applies to you, too." He chuckled and covered her hands with his, running his finger along the smooth gold band he'd put on her left hand a month before. "Well, Mrs. Hale, I'd like to tell you to go to bed, but your case study won't write itself." He lifted her hand, kissed each knuckle and turned to face her. "Can I help with anything?"

"This works," she said, pressing herself close against him. "I love you."

He smiled. Every damn time she said it, he smiled. "I love you." He hugged her tighter.

There were times Click still couldn't believe just how lucky he was. He had Tandy. He had Lynnie's place. He was doing what he loved. And Pearl was his. He and Tandy had offered to work out some sort of custody arrangement, but Georgia thought a clean slate was the best thing for her. Click didn't understand, but he didn't argue. Mr. Glenn had drawn up the papers and Georgia had signed them.

"What are you thinking about?" Tandy asked, looking up at him.

"Life." He kissed her forehead. "How good it is."

She smiled. "Are you saying you're happy, Mr. Hale? Even though you had to do the dishes?"

He nodded. "But I did have an idea. Something that might help wake you up, help you get your homework done." He cocked an eyebrow.

"Oh, really?" she asked, smiling broadly. "I can't wait to hear what you have in mind."

His lips brushed hers, trailing along her neck to nip her earlobe. "I'd rather show you, Tandy."

* * * * *

If you loved this book, look for more in
Sasha Summers's
THE BOONES OF TEXAS *series:*

COURTED BY THE COWBOY
A COWBOY TO CALL DADDY
A SON FOR THE COWBOY
And more, available now at Harlequin.com!

Get 2 Free Books,
Plus 2 Free Gifts —
just for trying the Reader Service!

HARLEQUIN®
Western Romance

As Hadley made her way toward the back of the store, a crash reverberated.

She heard a man's voice, followed by a high-pitched wail. Then a little boy yelled, "You made my brother cry!"

"Sam, I didn't— Tyler, don't… Boys, please!"

Momentarily abandoning her cart, Hadley peeked around the corner at the cereal aisle.

Boxes were everywhere. Among the cardboard wreckage, one boy sobbed facedown on the floor while another sat a few feet away, his eyes suspiciously dry. It took her a second to realize the boys were identical.

She cleared her throat. "Need a hand?"

The man whipped his head around. "Sorry about the disturbance, ma'am."

Flashing him a reassuring smile, she kneeled to retrieve a dented cereal box. "This hardly qualifies as a disturbance. You should see the library on story day when half the audience needs a nap."

He gave her a grin, and dimples appeared. *Oh, mercy!*

"What the heck happened here?"

Hadley glanced past Dimples to find a bewildered Violet Duncan.

The horizontal twin lifted his tearstained face. "It w-w-was a accident!"

"Grayson yelled at Sam!" the other twin accused.

Grayson…

Good Lord. Dimples was Grayson Cox? Hadley hadn't recognized her former classmate.

"I did not yell!" Grayson defended himself. "I told him to stop running, which he didn't, and then I pointed out the consequences of not listening."

Violet scooped up Sam and set him in the shopping cart. The action startled the boy out of his crying.

"If you and your brother will behave, you can come help me pick out something for dessert tonight." With a sigh, Violet turned to Grayson. "You want to finish restoring order here and meet us in the baking aisle?"

"Yes, ma'am." He ducked his gaze, looking as boyishly chagrined as young Sam.

When Hadley chuckled at his expression, all eyes turned to her.

Violet gave her a smile. "Hey, Hadley."

"Hadley?" Grayson echoed, turning back toward her. He blinked. "Hadley Lanier?"

She couldn't believe she hadn't recognized him sooner— or that she had yet to look away. *Quit staring.* Easier said than done. "I, uh… What was the question? Oh!" Her cheeks burned. "Yes. I'm Hadley."

Don't miss THE COWBOY'S TEXAS TWINS by Tanya Michaels, available February 2018 wherever Harlequin® Western Romance books and ebooks are sold.

www.Harlequin.com

HWREXP0118

Looking for more satisfying love stories
with community and family at their core?

Check out **Harlequin® Special Edition**
and **Harlequin® Western Romance** books!

New books available every month!

CONNECT WITH US AT:

Harlequin.com/Community

Facebook.com/HarlequinBooks

Twitter.com/HarlequinBooks

Instagram.com/HarlequinBooks

Pinterest.com/HarlequinBooks

ReaderService.com

**ROMANCE WHEN
YOU NEED IT**

HFGENRE2017R